Due North

by

Melanie Jackson

D1713478

Version 1.2 – April, 2011

Discover other titles by Melanie Jackson at
www.melaniejackson.com

ISBN 978-1461154723

Printed in the United States of America

Chapter 1: The Crash

Usually, when a plane falls out of the sky, it draws an immediate crowd. But not in McIntyre's Gulch, especially not in winter when it snows more than not. The last storm had lasted three days and screamed like the damned the entire time. A plane crashing would just be one more noise amongst a thousand others. Breaking plane, breaking trees, breaking thunder— unless it had landed on someone's roof, no one would notice anything until the spring thaw. Because no one in their right mind would be out walking where I was until at least May.

After a decade of finding odd things while hiking, especially with Max, this discovery didn't surprise me. That doesn't mean I wasn't dismayed to find an out of place something blocking my way through the high meadow. It is one of the few level places where one can look up at the sky, unimpeded by branches or rocks. It felt a bit like a cathedral, a sacred and secret place.

"Uh-oh," I said to Max, who cocked his pointy ears my way. "This isn't good. Someone has dumped their junker out here. Who would be such a pig?"

Max didn't agree that finding junk was bad. His eyes glittered with joy and he panted out doublewide breaths of steam. He was full of energy after his game of canine hockey. Max loved going out on the frozen pond and having me shove him over the ice. Kind of like crack the whip, but I let go and he goes skating. Unfortunately for him, I tire of the game long before he does. Max still had plenty of energy to spare for exploration and I felt guilty enough after my human hibernation to be lured deeper into the forest.

I looked at the giant white hump of misplaced something. Thick snow gives the scenery a certain sameness, hiding both landmarks and dangers, making it easy to get lost or fall into trouble. I had learned to trust Max to be my auxiliary eyes and nose. He always knew his way home. At least by dinner time.

Still, we had ventured out further than I had planned and were in an area I rarely visited after September since a passing glacier had left deep, uneven furrows that one could fall into if the ice wasn't strong enough to bear the weight. I was rather wishing that

I had stuck to my pattern and not found this eyesore, because now that it was discovered I would have to look into it. After all, though it probably was someone's abandoned piece of junk, it might be something— someone— else.

I began to circle the blob. In the right light, ice is more beautiful than diamonds. Certainly there is more of it, and with the sun shining on the crystals, weakening their bonds, snow can mumble and moan in ways that diamonds never would. Unfortunately, what was glinting at me was neither ice nor diamonds. It was glass. And from the general outline of things, I knew it was a sheet of glass, like from a vehicle.

A new fear presented itself. What if this wasn't an abandoned truck but one that had had an accident? What if someone had gotten stranded out here and then caught in the storm? I hadn't heard that anyone was missing in town, but maybe someone had come up from Little Fork.

"Damn." After three days of near whiteout conditions and below zero temperatures with a broken window, chances were anyone inside would be dead.

Max, inclined to rush in where angels and humans fear to tread, dashed up the mound and began digging at what might be a door. I hoped it wasn't because he smelled carrion. I love him, but he has some disgusting eating habits.

"Max, stop. You'll cut your paws. Now," I said and meant it. Unless I am very clear about what I want, Max is inclined to do as he pleases.

Max backed off reluctantly, shaking snow from his fur and growling at the mound which had clearly offended me. Three days spent indoors because of a late storm and left him seething with pent up energy and he was ready to tear that blob of snow into snowcones if that was what I wanted.

After the last three days I was too tired and cold to seethe. When the wind howls, Max howls, lamenting the time indoors when he might be out chasing snowflakes and wind and maybe voles. I let him out for short runs, but he is a social beast and prefers to be in my company— even if I am weak in body and prefer the indoors and baking bread to standing out in a blizzard like a proper wolf.

His choice would be flattering to me, but I suspect it is often about food and he doesn't stop complaining until I feed him. Day, night, he sighs and moans and whines. Sleeping is difficult with a dog that seems to sigh on both the inhale and the exhale.

"Stay back, Max. Stay." I scrambled up the slope and began digging carefully. The snow slipped away in soft crunches until I reached the inner layer of rime. The snow had melted on the hot body of the vehicle and frozen into a solid ice sheath. It took a few kicks to crack the icy cocoon and free the door of what proved to be a single-engine airplane.

"Double damn." I don't know a lot about planes, but no one flies anything less than a twin-engine up here in the winter, not unless they have a death wish. This had to be someone from down south who didn't know about winter in Manitoba.

Max, the big mouth, cheered me on.

As I feared, there was someone inside the plane. Only one someone that I could see, but he was past all efforts of first aid. I noticed longish dark hair, a crushed skull, a neck tattoo and hoarfrost all over the slender body. But above all else, I found my eyes focused on the large duffle bag full of money in the passenger's seat, and another one on the floor with a broken zipper that seemed to contain jewelry and some kind of bonds and stock certificates.

"Uh-oh, damn and damn," I said again. I peered around the body and looked in the backseat. There was yet another large duffle, though this one was closed. Maybe it had clothes, but since it looked like the other two and had what I thought was a gun barrel poking out of the tiny zipper opening, I kind of suspected that it wouldn't be filled with sandals and suntan oil.

"Max, shut-up please. I need to think."

Max turned it down a notch but he was still quivering with the need to get into the plane and explore things for himself.

I will admit to being a little paranoid and try to take precautions against it. Conspiracy theories thrive around here. Mostly because the majority of us have participated in at least one conspiracy, and sometimes more, though not always voluntarily. Paranoia is the cultural norm in McIntyre's Gulch.

Leaving aside the wildest hypotheticals about the plane and its occupant, even innocent bodies meant police involvement if

they were reported to the authorities. Bodies with money, guns
and jewels guaranteed prolonged police interest and might also
mean other criminals looking for misplaced items. I wanted
nothing to do with either.

Nobody else in town would want to talk to strangers either. I
should just shut the door and walk away. Someone else could deal
with it in the spring.

It was a lot of money though. A lot. And how would I
explain that find without mentioning the plane? There was no
way. In a town this small, one didn't have monetary secrets. And
once the story was known, someone might blab.

Maybe I was being too bleak in my thoughts. After all, the
plane had been out here for days with no one coming to look for
her. There hadn't even been any reports of a plane going missing
in the area, no requests for help at search and rescue. So maybe
there wouldn't be any trouble even if everyone knew about it.

And it was a lot of money.

"What do you think, Max? Should we go get help? Go tell
someone what's happened?"

Max gave a low howl at my euphemism.

"Good point. We shouldn't leave all that money lying around
where a bear might eat it. I better make a sledge though. It's too
heavy to carry. You can help me pull it, right?"

Max danced excitedly.

Building a travois is an easy enough task if you have tree
limbs, a blanket or tarp, and some string and a pocket knife. The
string and knife were in my pocket, the tree branches were all
around. The only trouble was finding a tarp, but there was a
canvas plane cover in the back, stuffed carelessly behind the seat.
The pilot was dead and neither he nor the plane would be needing
it again, so I cannibalized it.

Leaving fingerprints at the scene wasn't a problem as I wasn't
about to take my gloves off and risk frostbite, but I made every
effort not to touch the corpse anyway. The man, even dead—
maybe because he was dead— was repellant. Something about
that tattoo caused a bad vibe. And I watch "CSI" when we get
tapes at the pub. I know about DNA evidence. You can't be too
careful. I did look in the other bag though and it had a machine
pistol along with more money. The machine pistol wasn't

something we would use for hunting or killing anything around here. Except man.

Like I said; I'm a little paranoid.

"Okay, Max. Let's go to town— and no stopping for foxes or rabbits. I mean it."

Max raced away, leaving me to play oxen.

I didn't run. The sledge was heavy and the trouble with working hard in the cold is that it is too easy to overheat. That doesn't become a problem until you need to take a rest, in my case, somewhere around Potter's Ridge when I was breathing hard enough to make a fog around my head. If you wait too long, the sweat cools against the skin and begins to freeze. Hypothermia can set in very quickly. So, though I would have liked a longer rest and maybe some coffee and an apple fritter with butter, I allowed myself only a two minute breather before continuing down the hill.

Max would run ahead and then double back to check on me. After the ridge, the way became easier and mostly downward sloping, though there was less protection from the wind.

On a good day, I think of McIntyre's Gulch as being protectively cradled in the crescent of a majestic mountain range. That afternoon, from where I labored up on the ridge, I was thinking that the town looked more like it had been shoved down into a sinkhole and left where it landed. Certainly, it wasn't the kind of place a city planner would be proud of. Building sites were chosen because of flat surfaces that didn't need dynamiting and not design esthetics. There weren't many of those sites either and buildings crowded onto them.

I began following a deer track, figuring that it was proven passage with no holes or fissures hidden by snow for me to drop into. I also trusted Max to warn me if there were any other creatures stirring in the forest. He is pretty good at frightening animals away, even bears and mountain lions. I had a gun of course. You don't go out of town without a gun. But usually Max was enough of a deterrent. I hate shooting things.

"Brrrr."

The winds had died back some as we reached the zenith of our short day, but it was picking back up again. The occasional northern gust was violent, reminding me that we were on the tail

7

end of the dark season, the one that tries earnestly to kill you when you get careless or disrespectful of its power.

A flock of white-cheeked geese came honking overhead, silhouettes in a darkening sky. I figured that it must really be spring if they were coming back to the lake to scout out nesting spots and tried to take heart. Sometimes it felt like winter would never end.

Max barked and spun in the air, as if he really thought he could catch the geese.

"Silly dog," I said fondly.

Chapter 2: The Town

Town is small. Like blink and you'll miss it small. We have only four public buildings and a few private houses that line the one paved street. That's good because by the time I had reached our one and only flat street, I was grunting with every footstep and sweat was running down my face.

I was glad that it wasn't Sunday. The first building one encounters coming in from the south is a sort of church/town hall. It has a bi-monthly schedule for the itinerate preachers who look after our spiritual needs, weather permitting. The Presbyterian Minister, John McNab, has the first Sunday and the Episcopal Priest, Father White, comes on the third.

Most of us aren't terribly religious, but Sundays are boring in winter and we prefer not to be labeled as godless heathens by the outside world. It's a short step in most people's minds from godless to lawless. We keep up appearances to avoid talk. In aid of that we have bingo night every third Saturday when Father White flies in early for chicken dinner and legal gambling. Half the money goes to the Episcopal Church and half stays in town to buy things for 'the public weal'. Our last purchase was a new radio that replaced the World War Two surplus model we used for decades. That one had been moved to the grocery store. The radio is necessary because we have no cellphone coverage and only the landline that reaches out of the gulch is at the pub. Instead we are part of the General Radio Service. That's just like Citizens band radio in the United States. For in-town communication we have crank phones, relics from the 40's and slightly better at carrying sound than soup cans and string. Unless the lines have frozen.

Some might chafe at the lack of this modern convenience but it has done a lot to keep the town off of anyone's radar.

You see, what non-residents don't know— and never suspect because we all have red hair and closed mouths— is that while the carrot-top McIntyres are actually related by blood, most of the Jones aren't. We, the self-selected Jones of McIntyre's Gulch, are transplants from the outside; refugees, outcasts and sometimes actual outlaws. The red hair, in my case, is natural. Some of the other residents owe a debt to L'Oreal and Clairol.

We may have started as different people from different places, but through the decades we have become family in every way except the legal one, and we look out for each other accordingly. Sometimes grudgingly. But in the eyes of the law, DNA trumps emotional ties. We therefore tend to stay away from formal law enforcement, hospitals and any other institutions that might want to collect genetic data and use it to control us. Whenever possible, and it almost always is, we solve our problems, legal and medical, in house.

Yes, we were nearly as invisible as that enchanted town of Brigadoon, but that might change if we reported the downed plane. It would certainly change if the authorities found out about the money the plane had been carrying, though I should be grateful it wasn't drugs.

According to national statistics, McIntyre's Gulch has the lowest crime rate in Canada. We are also not much of a burden on the national health system.

Doc Jones (The Bones) is retired— or maybe stricken-off, if that is what they do to doctors who drink too much on the job— and takes care of most of our medical needs, including tooth extractions. I do his taxes for him since he is one of the few who actually still pays them. Fortunately for us, his common-law wife is a medicine woman. Linda Skywater only lets him see patients when he's sober and she is a wonderful practical nurse and healer in her own right.

In fact, our last outside medical case was an emergency appendectomy in '02. If The Bones had been sober, we wouldn't have farmed that out either, but he had gone up to his fishing cabin on a three day bender and Wings had to fly Madge Brightwater into Winnipeg. Linda and I had looked after her dogs while she was gone.

We have one other part-time resident who is not a McIntyre or Jones. Wendell Thunder is of the Brokenhead tribe near Lake Winnipeg. I'm not sure what brought him our way, but he has a sod-roof cabin just outside of town where he breeds wolf-hybrids. That's where Max came from. Wendell and I have a bit of romantic history that I do my best to forget.

A quick glance in the window at Doc's showed me that The Bones wasn't in. That wasn't surprising. He spent a lot of time at

The Lonesome Moose. If our town has an emotional center, it is the pub.

The first sign that anyone was still alive was at the market. Amy (The Braids— formerly a Jones but now a McIntyre) is married to Davey McIntyre and they run the grocery/post office/dvd rental store which they had inherited when Big Davey passed on two years ago. They also have a gas pump out behind the shop that is our sole source of gasoline and diesel.

I do their books too. Pretty much, if you have electricity then you pay taxes. If you pay taxes, I do them for you.

Amy was waiting on customers and they turned to stare at me as I struggled by with my burden.

One of her patrons was Surfer Jones. He was probably no more a Jones than a surfer in his former life, but no one knows for sure. He wears beachwear whenever the weather permits and talks like a surfer dude. He is also one of the few men who are clean-shaven. The rest grow beards in winter. I wish I could grow a beard in winter…. All I know for sure is that Surfer is a refugee from California and that he never actually lived near the ocean, growing up in a commune in Bakersfield. Surfer came north when things were heating up during the Vietnam War. He grows marijuana, eats mostly vegan, and uses his smokable to barter for the things he needs. He does not pay taxes and he has let his hair go gray.

I mouthed a 'slan leat' at them and Surfer mouthed 'dude' back. *Slan leat* is a Gaelic blessing, part of the founders' language which has lingered. It means *health upon you* and takes the place of hello in many conversations.

Danny waved. Danny (The Wings, who I mentioned before) is a Jones-McIntyre and our pilot. He makes a monthly run for supplies that can't be trucked in from Little Fork and handles our rare medical emergencies that need the hospital at Winnipeg. There is an airfield about two miles out of the gulch on the top of a flat mountain that can be used in summer when the lake has thawed, but Danny prefers to land on the lake or in town when he has supplies, and the road is just wide enough to accommodate him. If there's no wind or cars.

When he stays over in town it is with his brother, Fiddling Thomas. Thomas plays for us on Saturday nights at The

Lonesome Moose. The rest of the week he repairs things— radios, cars, whatever.

I waved a farewell to the three of them and they waved back. No one came out to offer me a helping hand. That was okay. I hadn't asked and we are big on staying out of people's business until they invite us in. Our mayor owned the pub and I wanted to talk to him first about what I'd found. And to convince him that, as mayor, it was his job to call the Mounties. If we called the Mounties. In spite of potential complications, I was pretty sure that we should.

Around town are a series of cables that are attached to iron posts. These are safety lines we use for getting around during whiteouts. We take them down in summer, but leave them out October to May. If a bad storm hits and you have to move around town, you need these safety lines to harness yourself. The whiteouts are deadly and we take no chances.

Finally, I made it to the pub. It took a final heave and a grunt to get the shredding tarp up onto the wooden walkway.

"You were a big help," I told my dog. Max barked encouragement as I backed my way through the door.

The Lonesome Moose has a distinctive look and smell. The scent of beer and grease from the fryer is inevitable in a small, closed up space, but layered over that was the odor of certain patrons that preferred to do their annual bathing during the summer months. Shallow breathing is a good idea when Whisky Jack is inside, which is nearly always.

No one will be surprised to learn that there is a stuffed moose in the pub. Any establishment rejoicing in the name of The Lonesome Moose should have one. A mere moose head would be commonplace, a whole moose, not so unusual. What we had is half a moose. The front half, which survived being eaten by wolves. It is mounted to the wall above the bar so that its front legs rest on the bar's wooden top, where it proudly stands on its two remaining hooves, eternally guarding the beer taps. The poor thing has begun to shed though and patrons have learned to accept the occasional stray hair in their beer. If we had any kind of government health inspections we would have to take it down, but we don't. And a little moose hair never hurt anyone.

Big John McIntyre owns the pub and runs it with the help of his daughter, Judy (the Flowers) who cooks, waits tables and always grows a pretty garden in the summer. I think Judy is a widow or maybe divorced. She is quiet about her year in Winnipeg and I think whatever happened there was not the stuff of Hallmark movie specials.

Madge Brightwater was in the pub that day with her bitch, Nakomas, and she greeted me cheerfully as I pushed through the doors. Madge trains sled dogs and races sometimes. There might have been trouble with Max and some of her team, but my dog is smitten with Nakomas so we had no doggy posturing.

The Bones was there too, but he was sleeping in a corner booth, head cradled in his arms.

"It's a little early for Christmas, Butterscotch," Big John said, eyeing my pile of duffle bags. "But thank you kindly for the thought, eh."

"Oh no, it's not." I unzipped my coat and pulled off my cap. The pub felt like the inside of furnace after the outdoors. "Only it isn't Santa Claus that's crashed up on the ridge."

"What?"

I leaned over and unfolded the tarp and then unzipped the bags.

"Mary, Mother of God," Madge breathed.

"There's a body too-- pilot. No snow gear. It's a single engine plane too. No passengers, no luggage. And it went down either before or very early in the storm. It was completely buried until Max found it."

Neither Madge nor Big John moved or spoke. They were staring fixedly at the loot. Like I said, it was a lot of money. And the gun looked pretty wicked, even to people who are used to firearms.

"And though I hate to bring it up, since it is a lot of money and I know we could use it, I think we had better call the Mounties and tell them about this. And when I say we, I mean you, Big John. After all, you're the mayor."

This finally got his attention and his green eyes turned my way.

"Now, let's not be hasty, eh? This is a lot of money and no wants to be bringing in the Mounties."

13

"I know," I sighed. "But the dead guy's clearly a criminal and this is probably stolen property."

"Aye, but maybe no one knows he came our way. There's been no reports of missing planes. I haven't heard of any local robberies either. Perhaps he's from Stateside and no one knows he's out this way. Mayhap we're safe."

I pointed at the machine pistol.

"He had weird tattoos. I'm thinking gangs or mafia."

"But it's a lot of money." John sounded wistful. "And if we call they will make us give it back."

"There could be a reward," I argued.

"I think we should call a town meeting," Madge said. "After all, this affects us all, John, and we need to be in agreement."

"A'right," he agreed, relieved. "And it's always been share and share alike, eh. We won't be keeping it all for ourselves. Start the phone tree, Madge. This is one of the few times that it will be convenient having a party line."

By the phone tree, he meant both the crank phone whose signal of one long, sustained ring meant that everyone should pick up, and the various radios people had in the trucks and cabins outside of town.

"When shall we meet?"

"We'll gather at seven in the town hall. There's a full moon and we've time yet before the next storm."

"Better do it here. I know it makes a mess, but it's warmer."

"So, it's still coming?" I asked, relieved that the decision about what to do with the loot and body would not be left up to me.

"Yep, and it's going to be bad for the delaying. You've firewood laid in?" John asked me.

"Yes, and fuel for the generator."

"Good. I've a bit of venison laid by for the werewolf." He smiled at Max. I don't hunt and Big John feels sorry for my dog who eats mainly kibble.

"Max says thank you."

"See you at seven, ladies. I'll waken The Bones," John said, picking up the duffle bags and heading for his office. He had a safe in there and I assumed that this was where he was going to store the loot.

14

Due North   Jackson

Chapter 3: The Meeting

"Would this gathering please come to order," Big John McIntyre bellowed, beating the heavy beer stein on the bar top as if it was a judge's gavel. "Please, would you all come to some kind of order, eh?" he pleaded when his first few, fierce demands went unheeded.

I sat on a stool at the bar by Big John's side, nervously nurse-maiding the now empty duffel bags I'd lugged into town. Why John thought I wanted them, I do not know, and I planned to give them back. I'd initially thought that Big John's plan for a town meeting was a good idea because I was sure that reason would prevail. But doubts grew and intensified as I observed the limits of his ability to control a crowd. We all kind of got cabin fever during the dark months and we got a little giddy when in company.

"Order in the court!" John finally bellowed, beating the mug on the bar top until it shattered.

This prompted uproarious laughter intermingled with more boisterous conversation.

Whiskey Jack remained huddled in his corner, nursing his free shot glass full of rotgut and probably wishing he had more. I hoped no one gave it to him.   A few more drinks and he'd get talkative and then argumentative. I would never muzzle my dog. Whisky Jack was another matter.

Compassion is a good thing, I know, and there was no denying that Jack had had a bad war. He came home with the twin convictions that he couldn't make it through the day without alcohol and that there was a thief under every bed. A thief that had stolen some cache of loot he'd found in the war and that I doubted had ever really existed anywhere but his mind.

"Oy!" Samuel Levine-Jones, only one of several odd cards in the pack, finally stood and called out. "Oy!" he shouted again.

For some reason, Samuel's irritating squeals drew more attention from the out of control crowd then had the most fierce rants that Big John could muster. Two more "Oys" and the group started to simmer down.

"Thank you, Samuel. Now, is everyone here that was asked to be here?" Big John wanted to know.

This, by the way, was everyone that could be reached by phone, foot, and radio. There were a couple missing faces.

"No," someone called out. "I think Denny The Diesel has trapped himself in the lavvy."

"He's not trapped," someone else called out in reply. "He's just having some wee private time with his laddie now that he's in a heated building."

And that's all it took to lose control again. Big John sighed heavily, dropped his elbows to the bar, and put his head in his hands. Given free rein, his audience ran wild. John wasn't mayor because he was a charismatic leader. He was mayor because he had a phone.

For my part, I'd seen and heard enough. Rising from my bar stool, I unholstered my classic, Colt .45 and discharged the cacophonous piece of ordinance into the ceiling. The result was complete and utter silence in the saloon, along with several drawn firearms. People looked at me with rounded eyes and I think mine were probably equally as shocked. Others have shot the ceiling before, but it wasn't a common act and I am usually the quiet, wallflower type.

"That's going to have to be patched," Big John observed, twisting his beard on his fingertip and looking up at the shower of debris falling from the ceiling onto his once clean bar top.

Finally there was quiet.

"*Oidche mhath.* Thank you for coming." Big John pursed his lips and shook his head, assuming a solemn disposition. His audience could see, quite clearly, and could guess from his use of Gaelic that there was some heavy news to share. "The young lassie, Butterscotch Jones, come dragging something interesting into town this morning. I'll let her explain, eh."

There was complete quiet as John abruptly stepped aside and I was forced to stand and address the packed house. Thanks a lot, Big John. I began telling my news slowly and steadily, though I had no real expectation of being able to get through my story in one telling.

"I found a crashed plane not too far outside of town. It must have come down in the last storm. It was a single engine plane."

There were whispered murmurs.

"There was a dead body in the cockpit."

17

Outright grumblings could now be heard.

"There was also treasure in the plane— money, jewelry and some bonds. Though I probably should have left it, I decided to bring it down the hill. Just in case. I mean, the plane might have caught fire, right?"

The group partook in a common intake of breath. Eyes began to shine. They understood the extenuating circumstances. We were all poor.

"We have it here in the safe in the back of the bar." I hoped that was true.

As I had anticipated, utter pandemonium erupted. People were hugging, and jumping up and down; screaming and beating each other on the backs. A couple old timers lapsed into Gaelic and began shouting clan war cries. Some wanted the safe opened at once so a count could be made. I had never seen such a scene. And it kept on going, no one willing to give up the happy moment to hear the bad news that they knew was coming.

"I ain't heard of no train crash," Whiskey Jack bellowed suddenly. "We ain't got a train, do we?"

"Plane crash!" everyone around him corrected but to no avail.

"Oy!" Samuel intervened when he saw that I had more to say and was looking at my gun again.

Eventually, there was quiet. This time it was an expectant quiet. We, more than most people, knew that there were no free lunches. Now they had to hear about the catch.

"And it's up to us to do the right thing— which is the legal thing— and give treasure back, or, of course, we could do the wrong thing and keep it for ourselves. But we all must agree on a course of action because there are risks either way. After all, people who have treasures and lose them are apt to also have friends and insurance companies who will come looking for it. This guy, maybe from the States, could be someone very nasty or powerful."

Again, the room burst into complete bedlam. I was pretty sure which side of the right and wrong issue the town was weighing in on. I heard Harry McIntyre ask his friend Billy Jones what he was going to do with his share of the money. Billy replied he was putting in a hot tub. This time, all it took was raising my hand to gain the room's attention.

"Leaving the money aside, there is still the issue of the dead body to deal with," I mentioned. "And the plane. It's hidden now but will stand out come the melt if anyone flies over. We can't move it, not without cutting down half the forest, and dismantling it would be a nightmare. And if we wait for someone to spot it from the air, there will be awkward questions about why we didn't call it in. It's right under The Wing's flight path."

The room began to settle down again. After a minute or two it was quiet. Everyone seemed to be in a state of solemn thought and contemplation, when Big John himself broke the silence.

"I say we call the Mounties to come collect the body, and keep the treasure for ourselves. After all, it's the fair thing to do."

Fair? I didn't see how he had arrived at that conclusion.

There were several utterances of "Aye" mixed with "Amen" and one "Dude!" from around the room accompanied by nodding heads of approval. A few looked unconvinced— and that would include me— but were quickly won over by their peers. The line about it being the decent thing to do for the deceased was especially effective in obtaining their agreement. We have all lost family and are not heartless, just avaricious.

"But what will the Mounties do?" This was from Judy the Flowers. "Will they just get the body and leave?"

"It was an accident. I don't know why they would stay. I guess it depends on if they suspect it was anything except a mishap, and I don't see how it could be." I shrugged. None of us was qualified to give accurate personality assessment of an outsider or their actions, particularly someone in law enforcement. Obviously, we have little practice predicting behavior in strangers. Wings was maybe more qualified than most of us since he visited outside town, but Wings also believed that aliens live among us— and I don't mean foreign nationals.

"Does this mean we can pave the main street this summer?" Amy the Braids called out. "The road is a damned disgrace."

"There you go again, wanting to expand your own front porch at the expense of what this town should really be focusing on," Harry McIntyre hollered back and everyone waited for him to drop the immortal line. "The needs of the good folk who live outside of town."

I met Wendell Thunder's eyes and smiled a little. This was an old fight and he refused to be drawn in.

This specific squabble grew into a much more general squabble between the in-towners and the out-of-towners. Which regressed, naturally, to a debate over who was an in-towner and who an out-of-towner. Ultimately, no one agree on anything that was said other than two things: that we should keep and share the treasure, and that we should call the Mounties and let them deal with the dead pilot in the plane. I made note of this and, grabbing Big John's arm, pulled him aside.

"Big John, I'm going to ask you to do something really important," I told him. "Again."

"Oh no, here it comes. I was waiting for the other shoe to drop."

"It's like I said before. I need for you to make this call to the Mounties," I explained, my expression serious.

"Why?" was his predictable response. "You know I'm not good with strangers."

"Because, I can't afford to get involved with the law," I declared, flatly. "I don't think my troubles from home followed me, but I can't be sure. You're the mayor. You have the phone. It makes sense for you to call. They probably won't ask for a lot of details anyway. Maybe they will just tell us to call the ambulance from Little Fork."

Big John paused in thought. I sensed that the crowd within the bar had also paused to watch and listen. It probably didn't take long for him to decide, but to me the intervening seconds stretched like hours. I was beginning to worry that I had already lost my case when he shocked me out of my anxiety with a reply.

"Alright, but you'll have to tell me what to say, in case they do ask questions."

I was surprised that he had agreed so easily, having no love for the law himself, and nearly said so.

"And you'll have to remember to say it just right," I warned. "I can write it all down, if you want."

"Daddy? Now what are you two up to?" Judy the Flowers interjected.

Before I could stop him, Big John spoke just as calmly and confidently as he did the last time.

"Oh, I just agreed to pretend that I found the plane and the dead body."

"You did what?" the Flowers said in surprise.

"And you need to call soon," I added, lest we start counting our loot and forget. "The plane can be seen from the air now.

The Flowers stood arms crossed and slack jawed in exasperation. I looked to Big John feeling of gratitude, even fondness, that I hadn't felt in years. He was looking out for me.

"Don't you think you should include me in such decisions?" the Flowers asked, sternly. "You've no more guile than a new laid egg. They'll know you're lying."

"Why, eh? I'm just doing my duty. And if I'm the one talking with the Mounties, there's less likelihood that somebody might slip up and mention the missing treasure." He looked me in the eyes and my cheeks colored. Well, he was right. I had a bad feeling about the money we had taken and would be happier reporting it and hoping for a reward.

"I suppose," Judy agreed. She really wanted a new stove.

Okay, so Big John wasn't looking out for me, but at least he was looking out for something. Self-interest was a good motivator.

"Thanks, Big John."

"Don't mention it, kid. And I mean it, don't mention it. Not to anyone, you hear me? Not to anyone at all. And you owe me a favor."

"I hear you, Big John." I reached out and squeezed his hand for whatever gratitude and fondness still remained in my weary soul. I was exhausted and wanted nothing more than to go home and have a long nap.

Big John would need lots of coaching though, and it was getting on toward eight. We agreed that having me stand beside him while he either phoned or radioed in his report would be best. Big John's reading skills were sketchy.

"So, when do I get me own share of the treasure, Big John?" Fiddling Thomas wanted to know. "I surely could use a new truck."

"All in good time, Thomas. All in good time," Big John assured the man, shooing him away from the office door where we were retreating. "We must rid ourselves of the body and the law first. We will also have to see about how best to dispose of the jewelry and such."

Before too many more embarrassing questions could be asked, Big John used his big booming voice for one last attempt to get everyone's attention, call the meeting to an end, and asking everyone to clear the room and to travel safely. The crowd continued to talk excitedly over their common interests and squabble over their common differences as they put on their coats and wandered to the door.

And just as fast as that, they were all gone. Except for Whisky Jack, who was still huddled over his drink and mumbling to himself. The saloon was empty and quiet. Big John took this opportunity to use the rotary phone on his desk and begin dialing. It seemed weird that he would know the number for the police in Winnipeg. Big John waited nervously for the connection while I coached him through his other ear about what he needed to say.

"Wait for the questions to begin or I'll never remember," he cautioned. "And don't lean over me. Look, I'll repeat them. You give me the answer. I'll repeat that. The result is a relayed conversation. It's as simple as that."

That really was simple but weird. Combined with his knowledge of the phone number I immediately figured that he had probably done this exact same thing a time or two before and I started wondering if Big John had another life that I knew nothing about. Like his daughter, he had spent some time away from McIntyre's Gulch.

The phone rang and rang. While Big John waited for someone to pick up at the Royal Canadian Mounted Police Headquarters in Winnipeg, we looked to each other in nervous expectation. This was the point of no return. I have always avoided the police, but we were, with forethought, planning on lying to them now.

Chapter 4: The Cabin

I closed the door behind me and Max yipped hello. Smiling, I knelt by the stove to light the fire and ruffle his fur. I always have a fire laid in the hearth, ready to start with the strike of a match. This is important in cold country when a fast fire might be all standing between you and death from hypothermia. It was one of the first things that Big John and Wendell had taught me.

"I need some hot chocolate. And silence. My ears are still ringing." Max flopped on his rug and grinned at me. He had had a good long run and was willing to accommodate my request.

What a day it had been— dead bodies, stolen money and endless arguments with my neighbors. It was the second most stressful day of my life. Still and all, it was worlds better than the worst day, so I decided not to feel sorry for myself. It was too easy to lapse into HDD (Humor Deficit Disorder).

And what could be worse than finding a body, you ask?

On the day that the bottom dropped out of my world and I had to disappear or get arrested, I was actually somewhat prepared for the parting. Not entirely of course, but more than the average person who might need to fall off the face of the earth.

For starters, my family— excepting my father— was gone and I was already fending for myself. I knew from the beginning that the guys I shared the dilapidated Victorian with were up to something that was maybe a little bit questionable and perhaps illegal. Definitely illegal, since they smoked marijuana sometimes. But since I needed a cheap place to live and off-campus housing was scarce, I told myself that they were just dedicated environmentalists, like the people in Green Peace, and that it would be okay to live with them until I found something else I could afford.

And mostly it was. Until the night that I discovered that 'like' Green Peace wasn't the same as real Green Peace. These guys were green alright, but peace wasn't part of their agenda. They wanted the United States off of foreign oil and were willing to go to extremes to make their views known. Those views apparently included the idea that the sincerest expression of belief was to get yourself killed, fighting for your cause.

The guys worked odd hours and were often away from home on 'green demonstrations'. About a week after I moved in to my little room, they mentioned how it was sometimes difficult for them to get to the bank during business hours and would I mind if they added me to their joint checking account and I started doing the banking for them?

Being underage, I had no checking account of my own and this would mean that I had a regular place to cash my payroll checks from the janitorial service and the pizza parlor where I worked part time. I could have asked my father to open an account with me, like most kids did, but past history had proven that I would be unlikely to enjoy the fruits of my labors if I let Dad anywhere near my money. Dad likes to gamble. On anything and everything. With anything and everything, including my college money which I had saved all through high school in a cookie jar in my bedroom. The offer from the guys seemed like a Godsend. And I felt I owed them a favor since they had taken to walking to and from my night classes whenever they were in town. There was a rapist on campus and they were protecting me.

The guys didn't drink often, just before they went off on one of their nature weekends. My roommates— let's call them Tom, Dick and Harry— sometimes threw themselves a little party before they went off to save the environment. Usually I didn't attend their revels. I was seventeen, on a scholarship that paid tuition and little else, and exhausted from working two part time jobs that barely paid for books and housing. But that night I happened to be home, happened to be in the mood for a beer and happened to get drunk on one beer because I never imbibed before and couldn't know that I am horrible about holding my liquor.

The guys thought that this was hilarious and let me stay with them while they were making fake IDs; driver's licenses and passports— Canadian ones. This didn't seem strange to me at the time. After all, underage kids always wanted driver's licenses so they could get beer and go to clubs and things, and trips over the border for cigarettes and medicine were common, Canada being right there and all. Of course, the guys weren't under age, but my reasoning skills had always been a bit hazy and I really was feeling that beer. I figured they were selling them to minors. Seeing my interest in their work, they asked if I would like to have one too.

And, God help me, I said yes. This was my second mistake (assuming that moving in with environmental terrorists was my first error).

They asked me who I wanted to be. That was easy. I had just read about a town in Canada where everyone had red hair. I looked for other stories about the place, but there were none. I couldn't even find it on the map in the library.

My own Bozo the Clown tresses had been the bane of my childhood. The idea of living in a place where everyone had red hair was terribly appealing. Like Shangri-La for a troubled teen. There were only two family names in McIntyre's Gulch. Obviously, one is McIntyre. The other is Jones. And since I am not fond of my real name (and you'll excuse me if I don't share it with you) I decided on the nickname my late Grandpa chose for me; Butterscotch.

A couple hours work and I had a Canadian passport. It said I was Butterscotch Jones of McIntyre's Gulch.

We had a laugh about my picture (I look pretty drunk in the photo) and I put the passport in my sock drawer and thought no more about it until the evening news the next weekend when I was eating my late dinner of cold pizza. The lead story was about an explosion at an oil refinery. A man-made explosion. Tom, Dick and Harry were named as persons of interest to the authorities and anyone having any information about their whereabouts should contact the police. Assuming that they were not three of the four corpses discovered in the ashes the next morning.

The guys didn't come home and I panicked. If I had not been my father's daughter, if Mom or my grandparents were alive, if I and my family had not had several run-ins with unsympathetic arms of the law, like child protective services and the IRS, maybe I would have done the normal, responsible thing that citizens do in these situations. But I am what I am, and a hasty but fairly thorough evaluation of my position— sharing a home and bank account with environmental terrorists that had killed someone— I decided that my best bet was trying my fortunes elsewhere. With some hazy idea about laying down a false trail, I sent a misleading note to my father's last known address, saying I was tired of college and I was hitch-hiking out to California to become a movie star.

25

Which I didn't really do. Because I had this Canadian passport and an idea of Shangri-La where they would accept a girl just because she had red hair and was named Jones.

Border crossings were different back before 9-11. No one looked twice at a young woman without much luggage returning to a small town in northern Canada. They might have been interested if they had seen how much money I was carrying in my fanny-pack. The guys' bank account had had almost ten thousand dollars in it, and heaven help me, I had taken it all. But I have an honest face and they never looked at me twice.

Thank goodness it was May. I would probably have died getting to McIntyre's Gulch if I had made the attempt in winter. As it was, it took me almost a week of hitching rides and flights to get there. And once I was in town, I was so tired that I wasn't in any shape for fighting off homicidal weather that rules six months out of the year.

I took a room at the pub. They have three that they rent out to the very infrequent tourist and travelers that need to stay overnight. Big John was delighted to discover that I was already a Jones, and having the reddest of red hair, he was prepared to claim me as kin. So were all the other Jones and even the McIntyres. There are very few young people in McIntyre's Gulch. People with families usually move away since the only other option is home schooling and there is no social life for children and little for adults.

They asked very few questions of me, just letting me rest up until I felt able to join in with local life. Big John found out that I had been studying accounting and gave me a job balancing his books. They— the Jones and McIntyres— let me move into an abandoned cabin at the edge of town whose owner had died the previous winter. Black Bart McIntyre had been very old and very miserly and not inclined to spend money on frivolities like electricity or generators, so no one else wanted his leaky old cabin anyway.

The first time I saw my new home, I almost chickened out. Though it was May, there had been a cold snap and the cabin was covered in cabin sweat (hoarfrost) inside and out, cluttered with junk, and smelled because animals had been living in it. But Big John lit a fire, and when he used some tar paper and shingles in the pantry to patch the roof, the place began to warm up and feel more homey. Big John's daughter gave me a mop and some cleaning products as a house-warming gift and we cleared away the clutter. The sun came out. Things began to seem possible. Even desirable.

And where was I going to go? I was just turned eighteen, wanted for consorting with eco-terrorists, and had a father that would probably turn me in for the reward money if I ever told him where I was. My burning bridge kept the fire under my tired feet and kept me running when any sensible person would have given up. I could learn to do without certain things like cable television and cell phones if it kept me out of jail.

Some conveniences were more necessary. I took some of my stolen nest-egg and got hooked up to the power, which is erratic, but nice when it works. I had a phone (a crank kind that was some kind of relic which only reached the other homes in town. Being the last to join, my signal was nine short rings). I bought a newer and more efficient wood burning stove that fit into the existing fireplace, and a back-up generator which everyone insisted (correctly) I would need in the winter. Oh and high-protein puppy kibble. A neighbor, Wendell Thunder, who raises wolf hybrids gave me a puppy as a housewarming present. That's Max.

Wendell and I have a little bit of history. We bumped pelvises a few years back, when I was too young and stupid to consider the consequences of a relationship gone bad in a town that small. Though it didn't work out between us, he is still kind of in the background, looking out for me. Mostly I appreciate it. I hadn't indulged in an affair since then. I have a lot of freedoms, but not sex without borders. That was part of my new not being stupid credo. Besides, though I am fond of them, I'd rather eat spiders than sleep with most of the men in town.

I don't have a regular landline at the cabin, though some people in town do, and we could have run a phone line from the pub. But the phones almost never work anyway and who would I be calling? Every friend I have left in the world lives right there in town. If there is an emergency, I rely on the phone at the pub or the town radio, like everyone else.

"Ready for dinner, Max?"

Max is always ready for dinner. I forced myself to my feet and headed for the kitchen (the part of the cabin that is not the living room or either of the small bedrooms or the privy).

At first glance, the decor in my cabin might seem a little hostile. There was a shotgun on the wall (mine), an ax (also mine) and a skinning knife (the previous occupant's but I liked the look of it and left it). The deer antler chandelier was also a little sharp and unfeminine, but it is good to have candles and oil lamps around when the power goes out. Running a generator can get expensive. Wood for the stove is free, if you put in the time and effort to collect it and keep it dry. I always have a nice pile inside, but it is hard to read by firelight.

I didn't have a lot of girlie things and no photographs of family. But I had a painting of Max that I had paid a traveling artist forty dollars to paint, a jar of dried celosia and amaranth from Judy the Flowers' garden and a small wood carving of a caribou on my scarred coffee table that Wendell had made for me last Christmas.

And there are books. Everyone in town brings me their books when they are done with them. And Wings always stops at the thrift shop in Little Forks to see what they have that's new. I stack them against the walls when I am through reading them. They make excellent insulation, though I had the feeling that they would not protect me from what was coming.

Big John had agreed to deal with the Mounties when they came, but that twitchy little extra sense that warns me when trouble is near was feeling restless. I had avoided the law for a decade, but I had to face the fact that my time for avoiding that part of life might be over. Once the law was in McIntyre's Gulch, there wouldn't be anywhere else to run.

Chapter 5: The Mountie

Horace Charles Goodhead, or Chuck as he preferred to be called, an inspector with the Royal Canadian Mounted Police, was having a rough time of it. He had flown in small planes, puddle jumpers, into the remotest parts of the Canadian Outback, but he'd never had a flight quite like this. First of all, it was winter. He never flew in winter. Secondly, he was crammed into the passenger seat with a box on his lap. He was astounded to find that the bulk of the plane was jammed to the rafters with supplies being flown into the tiny town of McIntyre's Gulch. Particularly objectionable was the assortment of cheeses that were left to ferment freely within the flight cabin. Chuck barely had room to scratch his nose, let alone search for an air sickness bag, which probably wasn't provided anyway.

The Mountie, a moniker which Chuck had always loathed because it summoned up images of that idiotic cartoon character, had stumbled upon the plane service while searching the Internet for flights out of Winnipeg. They were few and far between this time of year. Or, perhaps at any time. This was the only plane he could find that flew to his destination, a place he knew next to nothing about. There was almost nothing in the records about McIntyre's Gulch.

The trip was not his idea, nor had he volunteered for the investigation into an obvious accident, which hardly seemed like something for the Mounties anyway. But Chuck knew punishment when it was shoved down his throat. He had been a little too assiduous at his job and had showed his boss up when he had inadvertently demonstrated to the press that politics, and not ability, had led to his boss's last promotion. And maybe, just maybe he had been a little too enthusiastic about trying to improve procedures at the office.

Chuck remembered back to his last conversation he had with his boss, the one during which he'd been assigned this case, the one that hadn't gone well.

"You, Goodhead. Come here for second. I want to have a word with you." The Chief Superintendent looked miffed. Of course, he almost always looked miffed if there wasn't a camera on him.

"Yes, sir," Chuck said, coming to attention and saluting. He hoped it didn't look mocking.

"I wanted to talk with you about all those damned letters I keep receiving from you."

"All addressing important improvements including economies and efficiencies to be had within the department."

"Yes, yes. I'm sure. Look, Goodhead."

"Yes, sir?"

"I want the letters to stop."

"Sir?"

"Sir, what?"

"I don't understand."

"I want the letters to stop."

"Yes, I know what you said, sir."

"Good. Then see to it."

The Chief Superintendent began to walk away, then he turned back to fire one last salvo.

"Oh, and Goodhead?"

"Sir?"

"Since you are so interested in details, I have an assignment I'd like you to handle personally."

That's all it took and Inspector Goodhead was on a plane. This was the retaliation, an assignment to this crash site in the middle of nowhere in the dead of winter.

Regardless of the questionable merits of the case, Chuck accepted the mission with appropriate professional aplomb and dignity. The flight schedule didn't give him much time to prepare for the trip, and he was just able to throw together the needed belongings and race to the airport before the plane departed.

The pilot, one Danny "The Wings" Jones-McIntyre, had seemed dubious when the inspector presented his ID and insisted on passage. Nonetheless, he grudgingly accepted the surprise passenger onboard once he had extorted a fee that would have to be explained when Chuck turned in his expense account.

And then the bush pilot proceeded to make the flight a living hell for his reluctant passenger.

Danny the Wings was messing with him during their entire flight to McIntyre's Gulch, and Chuck suspected that it was actual hostility and not just a misplaced sense of humor that prompted these actions. The jokes were too cruel to be casual goofing off. There was the point at which they were flying over the Pembina Mountain Range and Danny pretended to be losing altitude. Then there was the time over Lake Winnipeg when the pilot sent the plane into a nose dive and screamed that he was out of control and they were going to crash. Each incident concluded with The Wings regaining control of the aircraft and laughing uproariously at his little joke, or at the Mountie.

Chuck tried to take it in stride, but things weren't made any better by the occasional sputtering of the plane and sounds like the engine had cut out, which The Wings assured him was normal— feathering, he called it— and besides they had two engines. What were the odds of both failing? But would the Mountie just look out of his window and see if any ice was building on the wing? Ice was a terrible thing and could happen so quickly.

Chuck knew the subject was just another malicious way to torment him, but he found himself glancing out of the window every minute or so, looking for telltale ice or frost.

In between aerobatic stunts and wing checks, Chuck was presented with some of the most majestic views of Lake Winnipeg and its surroundings that he had ever seen in his life. The Pembinas were spectacular and the unhindered snow white of the landscape sublime. Sunlight sparkled off the peaks and glaciers spreading a God-like aurora of light over the landscape. The Mountie found himself lulled into periods of enchantment in between the episodes of utter terror.

Of course, the genuine risks didn't begin until their landing in McIntyre's Gulch. The rest of the trip had seemed like a nasty game, juvenile but essentially harmless. Chuck soon came to question the pilot's very sanity.

"You know, used to be that all bush airstrips were laid right through the center of town where it was most convenient for everyone. Then lots of places started getting trucks and snow mobiles and once travel got easier some government lackey decided that planes should land outside of town, all in the name of public safety, which is a load of crap."

Making a sharp bank over a frozen lake, The Wings pointed out the tiny town lying in the lea of a large mountain. The site was hard to make out because of the snow and deep shadows. There appeared to only be a handful of buildings constituting the township of McIntyre's Gulch, most of them buried in ice which made their individual forms hard to discern. It was a desolate place and Chuck wondered what sort of people would choose to live there.

"But enough sightseeing. Best get on with it, eh?" The Wings said.

Chuck had thought that they were doing a flyover, perhaps alerting the townsfolk that the supplies were coming in, and then they would land on the lake where Wings assured him there was a kind of landing light and old World War Two radio beacon, but Wings made a nose dive toward Main Street, laughing as they plummeted toward certain doom.

Inspector Goodhead, though a calm man and in many ways a brave one, hadn't expected the landing to take place on the main street of town. Their descent between the buildings sent chills up his spine but fortunately tightened his throat until he couldn't actually scream. Adding particular terror to the incident was the fact that they almost ran into a rusty, old pickup that was in the process of rattling to a halt before the local mercantile during their landing. Only the driver's reflexes and a space between two stunted trees saved them from a collision. Regardless of the close shave, they touched down without incident, the worst injury being to the armrests by the Mountie's seat that now had nail-size gouges in them.

By the time the Mountie unclamped his cramping hands and clambered from the passenger seat of the plane, he was about ready to swear off air flight for a lifetime. Bending over in the snow by the side of the road to relieve himself of his hasty breakfast, Wings passed by behind, dropping the Mountie's single suitcase in the snow beside him and patting him on the back in mock sympathy.

"Don't sweat it, Mountie. You're safe now that you're on the ground. Just watch out for bears."

"You know, I could cite you for multiple infractions of the air safety code, not to mention reckless endangerment in your choice of landing sights. There are probably local ordinances against this stunt too." His voice was weak.

"Why, I rather doubt that. Don't you know that that's why we live in McIntyre's Gulch, Mountie? We never got around to passing those pesky air safety restrictions. Very few local ordinances about anything, so we don't have to deal with such city nonsense," Wings assured him, walking away to find someone to help him unload the plane.

Chuck would have argued, but he suspected that Danny Jones-McIntyre was speaking the truth. At the moment, he wished that he was not also bound by regulations because he would like to punch Danny The Wings in the nose.

"Hey, Wings," called a red haired man with an enormous beard that reached almost to his belly. "You got my Gruyere cheese this time?"

"Yes, and it stinks to high heaven."

"Good! I'll help you unload in a moment." The bearded man nodded at the Mountie but said nothing and Wings didn't introduce them.

Chuck straightened and drew in a breath of cold air, hoping the gastronomic rebellion was over.

As the view from the air suggested, the township of McIntyre's Gulch proved to be little more than a scattering of buildings around a main thoroughfare that was about as wide as a one way street and wasn't plowed nearly enough, in fact, maybe not at all. Chuck looked up from the mess that he'd left in the street to see that whatever citizenry there was on the makeshift tarmac were all staring his way, looking either amused or hostile. Wiping the bile from his face with his gloved hand, he stood upright, hoisted his duffle bag, and walked to the nearest building in town. This proved to be The Lonesome Moose, the local tavern.

Few of the scattered tables in the place were occupied. The first thing he noticed amongst the rustic wood planking was the entire front half of a moose mounted over the plank bar. Walking up to the counter, he placed his order in a slightly stronger voice and wondered if he had packed any aspirin.

"A glass of water, please."

"Water?" a tall, burly man replied blankly. He also had red hair. "We don't serve water in these parts. If you want yourself some water, step outside and grab yourself a handful of snow."

Several of the other clientele in the bar laughed at the bartender's joke. Chuck decided to use a little legal muscle instead of playing along. Retrieving his badge from his inside coat pocket, he flashed it and tried again.

"I'll have a glass of water," the Mountie repeated. "And two aspirin, if you have any."

The man behind the counter was large and bear-like, just short of being fat. Of course, Officer Goodhead was no lightweight himself. He stood six foot tall, but that left him a good six inches shorter than his counterpart behind the bar. He weighed in at 180 pounds of firm muscle, and that was at least 100 pounds lighter than the behemoth tending bar. The barkeep had wild red hair, as had The Wings and the other man in the street, while the inspector's hair was fair. The red on his head continued into the barkeep's wooly beard which Chuck assumed also matched the hair on his back and belly. The man was a model for Sasquatch.

Looking around the bar, Chuck realized that there were a lot of redheads in town. In fact, they were all red heads. Red hair is the rarest color among humans and he began to wonder how inbred McIntyre's Gulch really was.

Chuck tried to be pleasant and agreeable on the job when possible, but he would be willing to sacrifice manners to establish his position of authority amongst the strange locals when they were overtly hostile. And all over a glass of water. What was wrong with these people?

"Aye, water and willowbark it is," the bartender said, raising his palms from the counter to show that he wanted no trouble. Chuck had the feeling he was more amused than threatened.

The others in the saloon murmured under their breaths, no doubt complaining about the intrusion of some citified, badge-wielding Mountie into their rural way of life. Regardless, Chuck dropped his bag on the floor, had himself a seat on a stool, and took a look around the saloon while he nursed his iceless water. The handful of others in the bar glared at him warily while talking amongst themselves in low voices. Officer Goodhead couldn't help but wonder how many of them were planning his demise should he be foolish enough to step alone into the alley out back. And that was odd. Really, really odd. Some small towns were xenophobic, but he had never run into any place that expressed their hostility to this degree without any provocation.

"Say, you wouldn't happen to know where I could find Mayor McIntyre, would you?" the Mountie finally asked of the barkeep.

"Aye, that would be me, eh," the man behind the bar replied with evident signs of unease in both his voice and expression.

It was Chuck's lucky day.

"You're the one who called in the crash?"

"Aye, yeah, that would be me as well."

The mayor looked around like he was hoping somebody would interrupt them. Chuck's inner-barometer began to twitch. He almost always knew when someone was lying to him. "We didn't expect anyone here so soon what with the storm coming on."

"Well, we're surprisingly efficient sometimes. I've been sent here to investigate the crash site, gather what information I can, and report back to headquarters in Winnipeg as soon as possible. Mind if I ask you a few questions?"

Mayor McIntyre paused for a moment, looking decidedly uncomfortable. The others in the bar watched in silence as the interview commenced.

"Aye, go ahead and shoot. I mean, speak your piece."

"According to the report I received, you were the one who found the downed plane. Is that correct?"

"Aye." He was lying.

"And it was covered in snow since you've just had a heavy snowfall recently?"

The barkeep nodded his head as he kept his eyes turned away to the simple task of cleaning a glass that was already spotless.

"How was it that you were able to spot the plane if it was covered in snow? I take it that the location is remote?"

The barkeep thought for a moment.

"Well, I must have seen a piece of her sticking up out of the snow, hadn't I?"

"Aye, you must have. So are you saying that's what happened?"

"Aye." Another lie.

"That was very observant of you. Since it was a deep snow."

The barkeep shrugged as he tried to ignore the Mountie by picking up a new glass to clean.

"Look, do you mind stopping what you're doing and paying attention to our conversation? After all, I came a long way to see you today. The least you can do is show me the common courtesy of paying attention."

The mayor of McIntyre's Gulch looked up and shot the Mountie a hateful look that could have melted iron through its ferocity. Chuck wondered if he had pushed too far too fast. There was something damn weird about this town. He decided to keep on talking before his interviewee had a conniption on him.

"By the way, what were you doing out on the snow pack that day? The weather has been beastly."

"I was having myself a walk after the storm," the man said, awkwardly.

Chuck looked at the barkeep's well-padded body and had some doubts about him going out for a stroll.

"Do you often go for walks in the… what was it, morning or afternoon?" the Mountie asked, reaching into an outside pocket of his duffle bag for a copy of the report.

"Morning."

"Nope, wrong again," the Mountie declared, eyeing the report. "When you called in you reported finding the plane in the afternoon."

Mayor McIntyre's eyes shot around as if he was looking for someone to come to his assistance. Murmurings sprinkled with fierce words sprang up from the others in the bar.

"Mayor, are you sure you wouldn't like to clarify some of the facts in your report before we move on to the tougher questions?"

The mayor looked away again; obviously, something was chewing at him.

"Go ahead and tell him," a female voice called from somewhere behind them in the bar.

The mayor looked up and the Mountie swung around on his seat. What they both observed was a pretty young woman dressed in a wool skirt of grey and red plaid and a heavy, cable knit sweater the color of Irish oatmeal. She too had the shock of red hair which for some reason seemed to be predominant in this region, though on her it was pretty and her expression was less flushed and belligerent than on the men he'd met.

"Hello, officer," she said, stepping up to the bar and extending a hand in friendly manner that had so far been absent in the locals. Her gaze was candid. Too candid and his barometer began inches upward again. "I'm Judy McIntyre, known as the Flowers around these parts. Sorry I wasn't here to greet you in person you when you first came in. I was out back checking supplies."

"Inspector Chuck Goodhead, Royal Canadian Mounted Police," Chuck offered, shaking her hand since she was civil. She had a good grip for such a delicate looking woman.

"Well, Chuck, you'll more than likely be called the Mountie around these parts since local folk tend to refer to the job in preference to the person. We've too many McIntyres and Jones to do anything else. Don't take it personally."

"I won't." At least he wouldn't show any annoyance. No point in giving clues about his Achilles heel. "You could call me Inspector Goodhead."

"No, only enemies use titles and last names in these parts. Though I can't blame you for thinking we are hostile. No doubt my lug of a father made you feel as unwelcome as caribou in rutting season from the moment you stepped through those doors. We were just surprised by your arrival and haven't had a chance to dust off our company manners."

Mayor McIntyre had remained silent during the entirety of the introductions. At this reference to his manners, or lack thereof, he merely grunted and went back to cleaning glasses. Chuck offered a wry smile in response, charmed in spite of his wariness and certainty that there was more to this situation than anyone was saying.

"Can I offer you a drink? We can do better than water. Perhaps something warm?" the Flowers asked.

Chuck was left with the distinct impression that Judy was trying to distract him from what had quickly become a hostile interrogation of her father. He appreciated the gesture, but opted to remain on subject.

"Tell me what?" the Mountie reminded Judy. His voice was pleasant, his expression bland.

The Flowers smiled again and looked to her father, Big John McIntyre for support.

"Go ahead. Tell him," she urged. "T'was you who agreed and you who must do the breaking."

"I wasn't the one," the large man mumbled, somehow managing to sound like a scolded school boy.

"The one what?" Chuck asked, confused.

"The one that found the plane," McIntyre sighed, possibly in relief at finally telling the truth.

"Well, if you didn't find the plane, then who did? Why were they too shy to call themselves?"

"Well, the lassie has no phone and she's—"

At that very instant the doors to the saloon flew open and a woman stepped into the room. Though she wore a heavy parka, baggy jeans, and snow boots, Chuck sensed, possibly by her easy movements but more probably through wishful thinking, that she possessed a lithe, athletic body beneath the winter-wear. She had a head of beautiful, long red hair which fanned out across her shoulders when she removed her winter cap, shook her head, and strolled up to the bar. Chuck was awestruck. In addition to the gorgeous woman, though he couldn't be positive since he had been ogling her with all his might, he thought he'd also seen a large wolf come strutting into the tavern by her side and then disappear under a table.

"*Slan leat.* I saw Wing's plane. Did I miss anything while I was gone?" she asked, and then froze in mid stride as she caught sight of the stranger sitting at the bar.

"You're early."

"And he knows about you finding the plane," Judy the Flowers said apologetically. "But I told you Dad couldn't lie to save his life."

"Well, bloody hell."

"This is Butterscotch Jones," Judy said, turning back to the Mountie. "She can take you to the crash site she and the *cu* found. And if you're staying over, you'd best bunk with her. We've just had our spare room painted and the fumes would poison you. Perhaps you should go now. It gets dark early. If you need a phone, we've one here and so far the lines are up."

He was being gotten rid of. Again. Though the Flowers handled things more politely than his boss.

Butterscotch didn't gasp aloud at the effrontery of having her home offered to a stranger, but Chuck had the feeling she wanted to. He also remembered that *cu* meant dog in Gaelic.

"*Duin do bheul*," she muttered, confirming his supposition about the language they were speaking, and then called to her dog in English. "Come on, Max."

"Come back for dinner," the Flowers suggested. "We'll be ready for company by then."

The two women shared a look and Butterscotch nodded slightly.

Chapter 6: The Site

"Are you ready to go look at the crash site?" my guest asked once he had set his small duffle on the plank floor and looked around the cabin. His expression was unchanging but I knew the eyes missed no details.

When the Mountie finally spoke again, the tone was stiff and formal. Maybe he didn't like being fobbed off on my inferior stables when there was clearly room at the inn, and I could hardly explain that his early arrival had interrupted the Flowers while she was doing something she didn't want the Mountie to see. Like emptying the pub's still. Or maybe he didn't care for the cabin's rustic décor. Probably, in the city, they didn't use weapons for decorating. Probably they had carpeting and furnaces.

I tried not to feel defensive when I looked at my cabin through his eyes. Of course my home reflects my taste the same as anyone else's would, but you have to look harder for my personality than with most people's abodes because I must keep necessities close at hand. I don't think that the ice ax is the height of art, but I often need one to break out some mornings, so I have it by the door. And books are important. Lots of books show a curious mind, not an incipient hoarder. Any intelligent man would see that.

"Of course. Are you sure that *you* are?" I looked pointedly at his shoes and uniform which was wool, but not warm enough for anything more than a stroll through town.

A small smile lightened his expression.

"I have some boots and snow gear in my bag."

"That's good. I'd lend you some, but you wouldn't fit in mine."

"Heaven forefend," he muttered.

"At least you have a sense of humor. Most of your kind seem humor impaired," I muttered back and got a quick look. I said more loudly: "Okay, get changed. The spare room is through there." I jerked my head at the oversized closet with a cot that had once been a larder for raw meats. It didn't smell anymore. Really. "Oh, and guard your socks."

"My socks?"

"Yes, Max likes socks and feels anything off of your feet is fair game."

The Mountie and Max looked at one another. Max stopped chewing snow out of his pads and grinned impudently. I couldn't be sure, but I think the Inspector thawed a bit more. He was obviously a dog person. This raised him in my estimation.

"Clearly he's a hardened criminal."

"And unrepentant," I agreed sadly. "I am forced to keep the cabin tidy or go sockless."

"I'll remember."

I paced the living room, looking for ways to make it instantly more warm and appealing, while Inspector Goodhead changed clothes. There isn't a lot of space for pacing. The lower reaches of the cabin were built optimistically with large logs and stacked stone that made a kind in bench along the front of the cabin where I leave my boots, coat and scarf, but not socks or mittens. Mittens, being small and made of yarn were seen by Max as just being peculiarly shaped socks.

The inspector's room, the old larder, had been added later when Black Bart had grown disappointed and bitter and careless, and at first it required constant chinking to stop the wind getting in through the uneven and unpeeled logs that shed a little more of their bark every time they froze and then thawed. I had finally gotten tired of the leaks and bought a commercial foam to fill the gaps. Technology had triumphed over Black Bart's despair, but since it was a first effort, the patching wasn't neat or attractive and there was a slight petroleum odor.

At least there were no weapons on the walls and the old quilt on the cot was faded but nice.

The Mountie cleared his throat to get my attention and I turned from the small shuttered window where I had been standing, looking at nothing.

"Shall we be off then?" he asked. He sounded more at ease and was perhaps recovering his mood. I hoped he was an easy-going man. And maybe a little dumb and easily manipulated, though this seemed a bit much to hope for.

I reached for my coat.

"Up and at 'em, Max."

Days were growing longer but we didn't have many hours of sun left, so I hurried along the road without trying to play tour guide. Inspector Goodhead was inclined to chat though, so I was forced to be civil and answer questions about the places we passed.

The Mountie had a kind of stretcher sled that was designed to be pulled by a snowmobile, but unfortunately we weren't headed for any place that easily accessed. I let the Mountie play beast of burden while I carried the shotgun. The weight didn't seem to trouble him.

"Friendly town you've got here. I feel about as welcome as bubonic plague."

"It's friendly enough. If you're a McIntyre or a Jones."

"And have red hair."

"And have red hair," I conceded. "I think that's where your office went wrong. We are very suspicious of people with blonde hair. Maybe you should stop in at the grocer and see if they have any hair color. I'm sure people would warm up to you then."

"You're laughing at me, Miss Jones, but something has put people's backs up and I would like to know what it is. I should think that you would be glad that help has arrived so speedily. Since you requested it."

We stepped off the road and began climbing through the trees. It took some backward glancing to be sure the sled didn't get entangled.

"It may be the dress uniform that upsets us. Few of us look good in red so we aren't used to seeing it. It's our hair. The clash of tones— ah— watch this bit." I reached out and touched his arm. "The land out here is badly fractured and the light is getting tricky. It's easy to put a foot wrong. Let Max go first and walk in his tracks."

The Mountie obligingly altered course, following in Max's paw-prints.

"What on earth were you doing out here anyway? This is hardly an after-dinner stroll." The question sounded spontaneous and maybe it was, but I answered carefully.

"I was following the fur-ball. He'd been inside with me for the better part of three days during the last storm and he doesn't take confinement well. Knowing another bad one is coming, I decided to let him out for a long play. We went out to the pond for

42

some skating and then Max caught the scent of something and headed for Potter's Ridge. I think maybe he knew the plane was there. We don't usually come this way," I said this easily because it was true. "I thought at first that I had found an abandoned truck, but Max started digging and I could soon see it was a plane. I looked inside and—" I stopped.

"And?" Our footsteps were loud in the snow and our breath showed white as we forced ourselves up the hill.

"And I'd rather not look again." This was also truth, if not the whole truth. "Unless you need help with the body. He... ah... is frozen solid. There could be difficulties extracting him."

"I see. That is troublesome but I think I can manage. It isn't the first time someone has been frozen and I have proper tools." I couldn't think what to say to this and was glad when he went on. "Tell me more about the town. It is an unusual one. Do you have any residents that don't have red hair?"

He was a dog with a bone. I had to give him something.

"Two. And some people have gone gray, of course."

"And is everyone unfriendly and reluctant to talk to law enforcement?"

"Pretty much. The thing about McIntyre's Gulch, the families who live around here all have a need for freedom. For independence." To escape abusive spouses and unfeeling law enforcement, war-conscriptions or burdensome taxes. I stopped, trying to think of a way to explain without explaining. "The story is that the first McIntyre was a fleeing Jacobite. Maybe it's true. The pioneer spirit is still strong out here. We'd rather take our chances with the weather and terrain and wild animals than give up our independence."

"And you see life in the city as living in a gilded cage. And me as one of the keepers?"

He wasn't stupid. That could be good or bad.

"Yes. The city is safer in some ways. Maybe. But it's very regulated. Like a machine. It's all schedules and traffic signals and dress codes and rules, rules, rules. Out here, the only rule is 'don't be stupid'. Or you'll die. The act carries its own punishment. We haven't much need for outside law. And we don't really want the law trying to rope us in to doing things its way. Some of us have also..." I stopped. "Let's just say that some people's interaction with civilization has convinced them that not all officers are gentlemen."

"I see…. And the pilot was stupid?"

"He sure wasn't prepared. No survival gear, not even a coat. And a single engine plane, in winter especially…. This is someone who was either way off course or had done zero preparation for his travels."

"Forgive my curiosity, but given the town's sentiments, why did you bother calling this in? You could have just left him. Let the animals take him in the spring." The gentle voice suggested the brutality casually. I figured that I was being tested.

"I thought about it. We even had a town meeting to discuss what to do." I paused, wondering if this was too much information. I didn't want to lie any more than I had to, but that didn't mean giving everything else away. The Inspector let me think it through. I appreciated the courtesy. "The pilot may have been stupid. He was certainly unlucky. Maybe he had an instrument failure. I don't feel the need to judge. He's paid the ultimate price for his carelessness. But even if he was an utter moron, he might have a family somewhere, waiting and wondering what has happened to him. A family that is stuck with *your* rules that say you have to have a body to collect life insurance. It's a nuisance, but we did the humane thing. We are all hoping we don't regret it."

The stuff about the insurance was almost certainly not relevant in this case, but it sounded good. And if the pilot did belong to some mafia, we wanted them to know that the Mounties had been out and taken everything away with them.

"Not everyone agreed with the decision though?"

"In the end, they all agreed. We wouldn't have called you otherwise," I said firmly as Max came running back to check on us. "We're here. Watch for the darker patches of snow. It may mean there's a hollow beneath."

"This is hardly the pristine wilderness I was expecting, given the rough country we've traveled. This spot has been visited and recently."

It had indeed. I hardly recognized the clearing. Someone had wiped out my sledge tracks and churned up the virgin snow with a dozen pairs of boots and snowshoes. The damage to the plane was more apparent.

"I guess people were curious," I offered. Curious to see if I overlooked anything of value. "It's nice that they've dug out the plane so you can see it clearly. This way we can get the number off the tail. I didn't think to do that. I guess I was in shock." At seeing that much money.

"If this was a crime scene, it would be tampering with evidence."

"But it isn't a crime scene. It was a crash. An accident."

"Hm."

The sun was waning, the wind gaining speed and my bones felt brittle. I knelt next to Max and cuddled him for a moment. This was for my comfort, not his.

"At least there's no danger of fire," Inspector Goodhead said, looking under the carriage. "The fuel has wept out."

I nodded, just to show I was listening. He got up and went to the opened door. I kept my eyes averted as he searched the dead man's clothing.

"Did you examine the body?" The voice was no sharper than before, but I knew that he'd found something.

"No. I saw the wheel stuck in his head and he was obviously frozen and past help. I.... No, I didn't look at him. Inspector?"

"Please call me Chuck. I don't think we need be formal under the circumstances." He began taking pictures. "Did you notice his tattoos?"

"Not really. Max was jumping around, trying to get in the plane and I was worried about him getting cut on the broken glass. I just— well. He was dead. I didn't want to see anymore. Maybe I should have checked him for identification but I just couldn't make myself do it."

"That's understandable," he said gently, but he glanced at my shotgun probably wondering why I was being so squeamish when I was used to bloodshed of the animal kind. "Why don't you take Max away for a couple minutes while I get the body out?"

"Okay." But it wasn't. He had seen something that I missed. "What's wrong with him? What didn't I see? He was dead. I know he was dead. Please don't say you think I left an injured man."

That sounded both guilty and needy. The Inspector waited a long moment before answering. He had probably decided that once Bones had seen the body he would blab the details anyway, so he could risk being compassionate.

"He's been stabbed. It didn't kill him, but blood loss might explain how he got so off course."

"Stabbed?" I repeated blankly.

"Stabbed."

"Like with a weapon?"

"Yes."

Well damn.

"Are you sure that you can manage the body?" I forced myself to ask, wanting less than ever to touch it.

"Oh yes. He isn't a large man."

"I'll watch for bears then." Max and I moved away. I didn't see him pry the body out, but I heard him breaking ice and the sound made me a little bit ill. Even Max was subdued.

"So, there really are bears?"

"Yes."

There were some more nasty crunchy sounds. I hummed to myself and looked at the sky. There was only a pencil thin break in the clouds and it was turning orange.

"So, I can see why they call the pilot 'Wings' and the doc 'Bones', but why are you 'Butterscotch'?" The Mountie asked as he unfolded a tarp and began lashing it over the body, which of course didn't lay flat. When he was done I picked up one of the ropes and he took the other. We began pulling. It moved more easily than my sledge had.

"It's my favorite pudding," I answered at last. "But that isn't my nickname. It's what my grandpa called me." Not the whole truth but close enough. "Around here I am known as 'The Numbers'."

"Ah. Big gambler, eh? I could tell at the first glance. I bet poker is your game."

A Big gambler? Not hardly. That honor belonged to my father. I had gambled only once and that was because I was desperate to avoid the police. These days I play everything safe.

"No. I'm an accountant. I do taxes and such."

"So, I don't suppose there is lots of tax evasion out here? Lots of hiding spectacular wealth from the tax collector or anything interesting?" He sounded ridiculously hopeful and I realized he was actually teasing me. Maybe trying to put me at ease.

If he only knew. At least half of the town could be charged with tax evasion.

"None," I lied. "We've no fear of the tax collector. Mostly because we have no money. And haven't you heard? We have no crime in McIntyre's Gulch."

"Well, maybe you hadn't before." He suddenly sounded more serious.

"That crime didn't happen here," I said sharply. "None of us stabbed that man, and we certainly didn't crash his plane."

"No, the stabbing didn't happen here," he agreed, but I had the feeling his wasn't buying the no crime thing. I suspect he was looking at loose threads we'd left lying around and was trying to figure a way to weave them into a noose. I wondered what else we had overlooked. "Well, I must say that it all sounds rather boring for a policeman. That must be why you have none."

"Very boring," I agreed. "You had best leave at once, or perish from the tedium."

"I can't leave until the body thaws and we have a post-mortem. Bones can do that, I suppose. He is a real doctor?"

"Of course." Just drunk all the time. "You aren't taking the body away to be autopsied?" I sounded appalled. Because I was. I could have the Mountie in residence for one night, but not more than that.

"How? In Wings' puddle jumper?" he asked reasonably. "I doubt he'd care for that."

"We could get an ambulance up from Little Fork," I suggested. "They have an actual funeral home there. They could keep the body while it thaws."

"I doubt they could get an ambulance up here before the storm. I hear it will be bad. I may be here for days."

I looked up at the sky and cursed silently. He was right. I thought frantically about ways to stuff the genie back in the lamp and came up with nothing.

"Yep, it looks like you'll be stuck with me for a few days more," he said cheerfully. "That will give me a chance to really get to know everyone. I've never been in a town that has no crime.

It should be instructive. Maybe I'll take some valuable lessons back to my gilded cage."

I wondered how long it would take him to realize that we had no outlaws here because we had few laws to get outside of. There were only two. Keep your mouth shut with strangers. And help your neighbors when they ask, even if you don't like them.

"I'm sure everyone will be thrilled."

"Yes, especially when I start asking what was taken out of the airplane."

"Wh—what? Something was taken?"

"Oh yes. I'm quite sure of that. I don't suppose you noticed anything missing today?"

"No. I have been doing my best to notice nothing."

"Understandable. Death is unpleasant for the sensitive."

"It is unpleasant for anyone," I said sharply. "And you keep staring at my gun— like carrying this makes me a heartless killer. I'll have you know that I don't hunt. I don't like killing things. But I don't want to be eaten by a bear either," I said tartly. "We have wolves too. Max is great, but he's just one dog. Only an idiot would go out without a weapon."

"And the big rule is don't be stupid?"

"Exactly."

We walked in silence for a minute or two.

"So, do your parents live in town?" There was no reason he shouldn't assume this, but I had the feeling that he had already guessed that they didn't.

"Mom died when I was a baby and Dad— well, Dad might as well have died. My grandparents looked after me after Mom passed. They are gone now too." This was said repressively and for a wonder, it worked. I had some peace and quiet to panic in until we reached town.

"I am going to drop the body at Doc's— he's the house on the right? Big John has a fax machine, so I'll send in the pilot's fingerprints and see if we can get an identification from them, or the call numbers on the plane."

A fax machine? I had forgotten Big John had one.

"Okay. There is a fax machine at the pub. If it's working. Our lines go down a lot in the winter."

"Would it be untoward to ask you to dinner? It seems only right that I provide board if you provide my room. And it sounds as though they expect us at the pub."

I thought about dinner in the pub and how uncomfortable it would be for everyone. I wasn't thrilled with an evening of solo conversation though. I decided that it might be best to dilute our interaction for the next few hours.

"Do you think you'll be done with your work by six? We could meet at the pub. Maybe play some darts. They should have a good selection on the menu since Wings brought in supplies."

"Thank you. I'll make it a point to be ready." He nodded and then began hauling the sled toward Bone's house. He had no troubles with the weight. He had allowed me to help so I would feel useful, not because he needed the assistance.

I wondered what the doc would do with the body. Put it in the garage? His bathtub? How long would it take to thaw?

Chapter 7: The Mole

"Oh, hey, Brian. How was your weekend?"

Brian O'Shay was standing by the water cooler getting himself a drink as the typical traffic of the office passed. He gave it little notice other than an occasional smile and a nod as he quenched his thirst before returning to his cubicle located well back in the north forty.

Brian was a modern day veal, treated little better than the young cows penned in their stalls until the time came for someone to feed on their meat and bones. Only, in this case, Brian was housed in a cubicle, 8 by 8, which defined the entirety of his working life. He was far from the nearest window, and even if he put in another twenty years, he'd never have a window of his own.

Needless to say, Brian was not happy with his work at the Royal Canadian Mounted Police Headquarters in Winnipeg. As he walked back to his cubicle, he smiled at the boss's secretary. She ignored him, as usual. He couldn't help but think how he'd love to have that choice piece of meat working under him. He could definitely spend some late night sessions with her.

Back at his cube, he entered his password to reactive his terminal. As he did every morning, he performed a cursory scan of the active cases database looking for any new information that may be of interest. It didn't take long before he came across something that was very interesting indeed.

It turned out that there was a downed plane just outside the small town of McIntyre's Gulch not that far from Winnipeg. Brian read through the summary of the report and then sent a copy to the printer. He dashed to the printer so that he could retrieve his printout before anyone else saw what he was about. Taking the printout with him, he stepped out onto the balcony that overlooked downtown Winnipeg.

Though signs clearly marked that this was a non-smoking area, Brian lit up a Marlboro light and inhaled deeply. He performed one more quick scan of the report, ordering his facts, before retrieving his cell phone from his belt and speed-dialing an often used number.

"United Carryall Services, how may I direct your call?" a pleasant, female voice responded.

"Vladamir, 214," Brian responded, reciting the pre-agreed upon code phrase from memory.

Brian puffed at his cigarette and waited.

"Thank you," the voice said, and then there was a click and muted hum followed by ringing as the call was transferred.

"Speak," was the simple response he received after the second ring.

Though the voice on the other end of the line spoke only a single syllable, the accent behind that syllable was so heavy that it was obvious Brian was no longer speaking with a Canadian national.

"I found something in the active cases database that I thought you'd want to know about."

"Tell me," the voice said in a clearly framed Baltic accent.

"There's been a small plane crash near a small town named McIntyre's Gulch. It's not far from Winnipeg. The pilot didn't survive the crash. The report says that the plane was undoubtedly flying under the radar in order to not be spotted. Smugglers are suspected."

"How long ago?"

"The plane was found three days ago. An inspector by the name of Horace Goodhead has been dispatched to the crash site. He will arrive sometime today. He must have done something to piss off his District Commander to receive such a shit assignment," Brian speculated.

"Did they find anything inside the plane?"

"No. Nothing was reported other than the dead body."

There was an awkward pause in the conversation.

"Is that all?"

"Isn't that enough?" Brian quipped, becoming irritated at the lack of appreciation evident in the listener's voice.

The line went dead.

"Well, fuck you too, mister," Brian said, slapping the phone shut and reattaching it to his belt.

He took another deep drag on his cigarette as he tried to calm down.

"Hey, Brian," a young man said as he stepped out onto the balcony. "You going to the hockey game tonight?"

"Wouldn't miss it."

"Need a ride?"

"No, I'll meet you boys there."

The intruder was about to leave Brian in peace when he turned back.

"By the way, you're not supposed to be smoking out here," he pointed out.

"Oh, yeah. Thanks," Brian replied, dropping the cigarette and snuffing it out with the heel of his shoe. "I keep forgetting." You obnoxious prick, he wanted to add.

The interloper retreated back into the building and Brian smiled while leaning against the rail and looking out over the city. The information he'd just relayed could have put as much as 5k into his pocket. Who knows, he thought. Maybe he'd use some of that cash to take out the boss's skirt and show her a good time.

Brian laughed to himself as he reached into his coat pocket, retrieved another cigarette, and lit up.

Chapter 8: The Dinner

We were at an obscure table near the kitchen. No one wanted to sit next to us, but I could feel the weight of all the indirect attention we were getting. Half the town had turned out for dinner, even though the storm was due any minute and they would be heading home shortly.

I had had hours to come up with a brilliant plan to deflect the Mounties' questions but hadn't come up with anything. He had also beaten me in straight sets at darts.

"Why are you here?" I asked Inspector Goodhead— Chuck, I mean. The informality was not coming naturally, though I found that I had a reluctant liking for my uninvited guest. There I was, sitting down to dinner with an officer of the law and not even thinking of running away. It was a first. Let's hear it for personal growth.

He blinked.

"You called me to the crash."

"No, I mean, why you? We didn't know about the stabbing when we called. We didn't ask for an inspector, just someone to get the body and give it back to his family. They don't usually send inspectors to accidents, do they?"

"Ah," he cleared his throat. "Generally speaking, that is true. I fear that this time it's a matter of revenge."

"On us?" I asked, confused.

"No, on me. I embarrassed my boss and made him look like an idiot. On the evening news. And perhaps I suggested a few too many ways that he could improve department efficiency. At the moment I am *persona non grata.*"

"Is he an idiot?" I asked curiously.

"He's my superior," Chuck said sternly.

"I rather doubt that," I muttered and we shared a rare, small smile.

Why did I like him? There was no future in it and a lot of danger.

"Do you think this establishment runs to wine?" Chuck asked.

"Yes, with screw tops mostly," I warned him.

"Should we risk it?"

53

"Not on my account. I don't drink."

"Puritanism?" he guessed.

"No, low alcohol tolerance. Half a glass and I'd be out skinny-skiing or something dumb."

"And that would be a bad thing?"

"In this weather? With you around ready to arrest me for drunk and disorderly?"

"A man can only hope."

He was teasing me again. It left me feeling baffled. It didn't match his rather by-the-book manner he used most of the time.

"I'm guessing there are no liquor laws here."

I shrugged.

"No children here, so it doesn't matter as much. And we never went dry, even when the rest of Manitoba did." This was back in 1921 when prohibition fever came up from the States and swept over the northern continent. We not only hadn't gone dry, McIntyre's Gulch had become a large producer of illegal spirits. We still made our own whiskey.

"No children. That would be a little strange. Sad too."

I shrugged.

"People go away to have kids, but some come back later."

The Mountie shook his head.

"You seem strange to me too. I think that you must be a little different from other people. To do this job." I shook my head back at him as he glanced around the pub, thinking that of course he was different. We were all kind of weirdos here in McIntyre's Gulch. "I mean this nicely, but detectives must be a bit like gossip columnists or the paparazzi."

"I beg your pardon." Now he looked startled.

"I mean, to have the deep urge to know things about other people who are strangers and to pursue it doggedly, that's not normal. And then to maybe go ahead and use the knowledge you dig up, even when it would be better to let sleeping dogs lie. It takes a certain kind of person to do that." I tried to explain what I was feeling in terms less insulting. "I know that the truth is supposed to be some kind of higher god that sets us free, but what is truth? Unless we're talking Divine truth, it's just statistics and opinion and personal bias. And in your line, no one gets set free.

People must be very uncomfortable around you. Why would anyone do what you do?"

It was his turn to shrug. The question was easy to phrase, but the answer had to be complicated.

"So, you think truth doesn't matter?" he asked at last.

The Mountie was bound by occupation to lobby for truth in the name of justice but was smart enough to realize that I probably was not his target demographic.

"Not if the truth hurts innocent people. It would be different if you could stop a bad thing from happening, but what is the point of knowing stuff when it's all over and done with and the truth will just do harm to those who are left in the ruins?"

"Give me an example."

"Well, a rape victim that didn't want what happened to be known. Didn't want her face in the papers."

I got a long look and hoped I hadn't started him thinking about my past.

"So, you would want me to pretend that that I didn't notice that something had been dragged away from the crash site?" He sounded so reasonable.

"I'm not saying anything was dragged from the crash site—"

"I am."

"But if there was, maybe there was a reason for it. Maybe there's a higher purpose than truth at work sometimes." There probably wasn't in most cases and certainly not in this one. Except that we were possibly cosmically entitled to some remuneration for the minimal taxes we paid the government every year, since we got no services from the state.

"There's always a reason for people to do things, Butterscotch. Even horrible things," he said kindly. "Drug addicts steal because they hurt and need drugs. That doesn't make it right. And catching them before they steal again keeps them from harming more people."

"Drugs? You think there were drugs?" I demanded, diverted. I hoped my mouth wasn't hanging open.

"No drugs?"

"No—" I stopped myself. "Not that I saw."

"Probably no under-aged prostitutes headed for the brothel?"

"Good God, no!" I made myself lower my voice when the other guests' eyes turned my way. I waved a hand at Fiddling Thomas who looked ready to come over to the table. Thomas is lovely, but hot-tempered. "Though if we had found one— even if she was an illegal— I probably would hide her. Or him. If they asked." I took a swallow of my ginger ale. "So, you think the pilot was a really bad person? Someone up to no good?"

"I know he consorted with really bad people and got himself stabbed."

"Did you get an ID on him?"

"Yep. Records are sketchy, but he's Russian mafia down in The States and has a long rap sheet. The FBI has been looking for him."

Oh damn. That's all we needed. I drank more ginger ale and hoped that the Flowers would bring us our burgers soon. You can't talk when your mouth is full.

"That fact is almost as interesting as what I didn't find."

"What's that?" I asked, but I had a bad feeling. The shelf life on suspicion and paranoia in McIntyre's Gulch is a lot longer than for canned goods. A curious Mountie and a fax machine. Anything could happen. I braced myself.

"There is no record of birth for a Butterscotch Jones."

"Of course not," I said with an ease I was definitely not feeling. "I doubt any births were recorded in town before The Bones got here. People here have always used a midwife or medicine woman and they aren't big on paperwork. And I changed my name years ago."

The Mountie blinked.

"Look. It isn't that big a mystery. My father gambles— or gambled. He may be dead now. As you can tell, there isn't much scope for a gambler in McIntyre's Gulch or even Manitoba, so my mother foolishly eloped with him and went off to live his dream. When she died, Dad discovered what a burden a kid is and dumped me on my grandparents before taking took off to find brighter lights and bigger cities in the United States. Years passed between visits. We weren't close." I was condensing history for convenience and not mentioning how my dad would drop around periodically and threaten to take me away if my grandparents didn't pay him off. Not that he had actually taken me in when they died. I would have ended on the streets if not for my various grants and the housing arrangement with Tom, Dick, and Harry. "Last I heard, he was in Nevada and in debt to the kind of people you don't want to be indebted to. That was right after he stole my college money— though I guess it isn't stealing since I was a minor and the law would say he was entitled to anything I earned." This came out rather bitterly.

"So, you haven't seen him recently?" I am almost sure that there was sympathy there, but I can do math— dead pilot, mob tattoos, gambling father. It was a tenuous connection, but a connection nonetheless. And he'd give birth to kittens if he found out that my father had been of Russian extraction.

"Not in a decade. And, as I said, he may be dead. And, in case you have suffered a sudden drop in IQ and intuition, yes, I like my neighbors more than I liked him. For that reason I let the past stay in the past— and that includes a name that meant nothing to me even when I bore it. I like my present, no matter how humble it may seem to you, and I don't want to ruin it with bad memories. I am Butterscotch Jones of McIntyre's Gulch."

"I don't suppose you would care to share your old name anyway?"

"I would not. It isn't relevant. It has nothing to do with crashed planes and I'm not that person anymore. And—" I smiled maliciously, "—no one here knows my dad's name either since I changed it before I came to— *back*— so there is no point in asking."

"Is that meant to challenge me?"

"It's meant to keep you out of my business." I didn't hide my exasperation.

"Do you think it will work?" he asked curiously.

"I sincerely hope so. Or this will be the shortest friendship in history."

He looked thoughtful but made no promises.

I gulped more ginger ale and then crunched some ice when the liquid was gone. The tentacles of my past were still with me, weakened maybe, but not gone. And it was the same for many Jones in town. This man was— though smart and likable— our enemy.

And all he had to do to catch us was to wait and watch for someone to put a foot wrong. One misstep by me, or anyone, and we might all be betrayed, our sanctuary exposed. The betrayal would be accidental, I was sure. Pretty sure. But that wouldn't be much consolation for those of us who had run to the ends of the earth and had nowhere else left to go.

Though I rarely think about it, and therefore don't go looking for it in others, I wondered how many of my neighbors resented being driven to their last stand. Did they harbor resentment for those who put them here and long to escape back into their old lives? I had chosen this life, but what of those born to it? Did they wish that they could move on to bigger and better things? I was so grateful to have escaped jail that I felt little envy for anyone on the outside, but did others in McIntyre's Gulch count their blessings and come up short?

As a for instance, I was pretty sure that Whisky Jack was over at the bar demanding money from Big John. His addled brain probably believed that the money actually was his and he was never satisfied.

"Don't frown. Your neighbors respect and like you too. They speak highly of your intelligence. I asked about you by way of breaking the ice and they were all complimentary. Especially Madge Brightwater."

I nodded, shoving those nasty tentacles aside. I forced a smile.

"Madge wants me to get married. She probably also told you that I can cook and have the wiles of Mata-Hari."

"Cooking was mentioned," Chuck admitted. "But it went deeper than that. She said you are one of the few people she trusts with her dogs. This is a high sign of respect."

"That's true. But Madge would think a two-headed cannibal was a good person if her dogs liked them."

Chuck shook his head at me, but I am not comfortable accepting compliments and probably never will be. My grandma used to say that praise to the face was open disgrace. She had lived in Maine, but would have done well in McIntyre's Gulch.

"Respect is good, but tolerance for one another's faults is absolutely critical in a place this small. We have to rely on each other for skills we don't have, so we tend to be grateful for our neighbors, warts and all. Dependence can be a stronger bond even than friendship, you know."

Chuck nodded.

"I can see that. It's the same in police work."

I nodded.

"So, I am going to give you a chance to demonstrate some of that intelligence your neighbors credit you with. Why don't you tell me what's really going on with the plane? Maybe I can help. My job isn't just about chasing bad guys, you know. It is also about protecting honest citizens."

And there was the rub.

"Excuse me," I said, my eyes flicking over to the bar and not liking what I was seeing. "I had better check on our food."

I got to my feet and headed for the bar. As I feared, Whisky Jack was whining to Big John about getting his money. Our town drunk was the exception to the rule and he was never satisfied. I think that it was this soul-deep dissatisfaction that drove him to drink as much as memories of the war.

"*Slan leat*. Big John, might I have a moment?" My voice was sharp enough to cut across Whisky Jack's grumbles.

"Sure, Butterscotch. Let's step into my office. It's more private, eh."

I waited for the door to close and when I spoke, it was in a low voice that couldn't be overheard even by someone with an ear to the keyhole.

"The Mountie says that the pilot was Russian mafia and that he knows that things are missing from the plane. He's thinking drugs. The FBI is looking for the pilot too."

"Drugs." Big John looked unhappy. "And the FBI." The FBI was supposed to work inside the borders of the USA but they had strong ties to Canada and would have no trouble getting cooperation over the border.

"The only thing worse for us would be terrorists. Let's give back the bonds and things. And the jewels. We don't know how to fence them and we would probably get caught if we tried. We can pack up a duffle, drop it in the forest near the plane and let the Mountie discover it when I take him hiking. Then he has found a nice accidental death, recovery of some of the stolen property with a reasonable doubt that the rest was lost in the crash. Case closed and he goes home happy and writes a report. He doesn't investigate everyone in town looking for drug dealers. He doesn't bring in more Mounties."

Big John frowned.

"We keep the money and the gold that we can melt?"

"Yes— but we put the gun in the bag too. It was probably used in a dozen crimes and they can match it with ballistics. It would be bad for any of us to get caught with it."

"I might be agreeable, but we would have to have another meeting."

I groaned.

"Can we do that while he's here?"

"Maybe. You better get back out there, eh? Don't want Whisky Jack talking to the Mountie. That man is going to be trouble."

No, we didn't want the two of them talking, though I wondered if John was referring to the Mountie or to Whisky Jack when he spoke of trouble.

I returned to our table. The venison burgers had arrived along with a lot of side-dishes we hadn't ordered.

Chuck smiled at my astonishment.

"A bribe, do you think? Or an effort to keep me preoccupied?"

"Nonsense, just small-town friendliness. I always order French fries, onion rings and, um, brown gunk on... chips?"

"Nachos, I think."

"Oh. Yes, I always have those."

"Any luck convincing The Mayor to see reason?" Chuck asked, opening the ketchup bottle.

"I live in hope. Perhaps you should try prayer," I said, opening my hamburger and extracting the slices of turnip. I don't know why the Flowers puts it on the burgers. No one likes turnip, raw or grilled, and it isn't like it actually fakes us into thinking we have ripe tomato.

"And you wouldn't dream of confiding in me on your own?"

I hadn't come up with an answer to the Mountie's question when the door to the pub blew open. Caught by the wind, it threw the muscular stranger holding the latch into the room and slammed the door into the wall. The other man behind him entered in a more conventional manner, but his capped head was tucked against the rising wind and the snow that swirled around him.

Strangers in any number are rare and, being paranoid, I felt the small hairs on my neck rise even before they looked up and I saw their unsmiling faces. These were the perfect caricatures of villains. Except that in one I saw a capacity for very real violence. I am sure that color drained from my face, but being winter pale already, perhaps Chuck didn't notice.

Chuck didn't like what he saw either and straightened. He reminded me of Max when he saw prey. I half expected the new arrivals to stalk up to our table, whip out handguns and demand we hand over the money from the airplane, but instead they looked around the room in an assessing manner and then one approached the bar.

Chuck leaned across the table and took my hand. The grip wasn't harsh but it wasn't lover-like either. His voice was low but clear enough for me to hear his words even above the renewing chatter of the other patrons.

"The Russians have arrived— and I don't mean the Moscow Ballet Company. Now might be a really good time for you to tell me exactly what was in that plane."

Chapter 9: The Russian Mafia

Grigori Dimitri Smirnoff lit up a cigarette and inhaled deeply. It was an off-the-shelf, American cigarette, though it came from a silver, European case. A full flavored brand, rather than one of those 'lights' the Americans tended to smoke. Exhaling lavishly, he tried to blow away his irritation.

In response to a telephone conversation he'd had with a highly placed mole at RCMP Headquarters, Grigori had boarded a private Lear Jet left idling on an undisclosed runway in New Jersey. Once airborne, the jet began a nonstop flight to some insignificant suburb of Winnipeg known as McIntyre's Gulch, Manitoba, Canada.

Canada. In winter.

Grigori was not a happy man. This was true most of the time; this state was just more prominent at the present. Grigori never wanted to fly north before spring. For one thing, he didn't like snow. It reminded him too much of Siberia, a time in his life he'd rather forget. For another? Well, he didn't like snow a lot.

The powerful jet Gregori was riding through the stratosphere at seven-hundred-fifty kilometers per hour purred like a barely restrained beast. He respected the feel of the twin jet engines that vibrated through the armrest of his seat. If nothing else, Grigori Dimitri was all about power. In all other respects, he despised air travel.

Grigori swiveled ever so slightly as he rocked in his premium, business class, leather clad seat, unable to contain the pent up anxiety that he'd brought with him from his last phone conversation. He really couldn't explain his own agitation at times. This being one of them. Perhaps it had simply been too long since he'd killed a man. Perhaps he was anxious about getting their belongings back, as were the five other men sitting in the spacious cabin with him, if they were smart. There could be a great deal of trouble for Grigori if they did not get the merchandise back, and trouble was the only thing he was generous about sharing.

They'd been in flight from New Jersey for several hours now trying to fly around an approaching storm. Though it was becoming dark, the lights from the ground had grown steadily more scarce until there were no more to be seen. Grigori took this as a good sign, assuming that they had finally entered Canadian airspace. It couldn't be much longer before they touched down at the town's airfield and entered the nearest bar so they could have a lager. And they needed to begin preparations to recover the missing items. About the body, he cared nothing at all.

Grigori considered the other men surrounding him in the passenger compartment. He knew that he could drink any or all of them under the table, but which of them could he trust to be there by his side, prepared to do as he was told, when the time came? Alexei and Ivan were the brothers from Kiev, two cousins foisted upon him by his own brother. One a dreamer, the other a lover. Neither would be worth shit in a fight. Not even Sasha was ideal for this task, come to that. Though he was big as an ox, he was as dim as one too, and Grigori doubted he'd be willing to do what it took to win, even if Sasha did bare the impressive moniker The Butcher of Minsk.

Bah, butcher, Grigori mused. In the days of Stalin; now, those were butchers.

Then there was the one who joked all the time, Misha. How Grigori already wanted to wring his neck and shut up his laughter forever.

Nope, the only man he needed either standing by his side or lying beneath his feet in the end was Anatoli, the leader of this worthless pack of rabble and the man currently piloting the plane. Anatoli had steel and wit. He was definitely the one to keep in check, and on a short leash. He was a good weapon, but one that could be turned on Grigori, who could have flown the plane himself except that it suited his dignity to make someone else do it.

As for Anatoli, aware of his boss's impatience, he was keeping track of Gregori in return. After all, though the pay was good, the man had a bad reputation. And ever since they'd met, Gregori had done all he could to try to live down to that bad reputation. Anatoli both despised and feared the man— a crude form of respect favored and therefore cultivated by Grigori.

"Anatoli, what time do we arrive?" Gregori demanded.

"Within minutes, Comrade Colonel," Anatoli replied, intentionally showing deference in his decision to dredge up an old title.

"And the condition of the airfield?"

"Frozen."

"Frozen?"

"You see, it's not exactly an airfield, Comrade Colonel." Anatoli hesitated, and then relayed the bad news. "It's more of a small lake."

"You're landing this jet on a lake?"

"Yes. It should bear the weight until mid-spring."

Surely we'll be out before then, Anatoli thought; but then, he had never received a time table from the man so obviously in charge of the mission. He was simply ordered to pack for the cold and be ready at the airport. Anatoli held his breath waiting for the next verbal barb to strike from the Colonel in the rear of the plane. Instead, Gregori directed his ire to one of the pair of brothers, the kids— Anatoli could never tell them apart.

"You know that our Colonel is a homicidal maniac?" Misha asked in a low, conspiratorial tone.

"I've heard rumors," Anatoli confided with a nod of his head.

"Oh? So, you've heard rumors, have you? And have you heard the one about the Colonel who worked in the basement of KGB prisons at Lubyanka?"

"We've all heard rumors and stories, but I've seen no evidence," Anatoli countered. "Anyway, no one could be as bad as the man in the stories I've been told. Not even Sasha."

"Bah, Sasha! The Butcher of Minsk," Misha mocked. "Just because no one takes the time to find out that he was a butcher in Minsk. That's why when we went looking for the famed Butcher of Minsk, everyone in Minsk directed us to Sasha, the sausage stuffer. The poor man. I think he's sometimes overwhelmed by the burden of his own misbegotten, bad reputation."

"Believe me, Sasha has lived up to his reputation, deserved or not, since joining the organization," Anatoli countered, defensively.

"He tries, but his heart just isn't in it," admitted Misha. "Hey, speaking of heart, what's up with you and the heavenly young woman I saw you with at the club last weekend?"

"Oh, that," Anatoli responded, offhandedly. "That was nothing at all."

Admittedly, to Anatoli— a young, virile man with needs— the encounter with the heavenly young woman last weekend had meant much more to him than nothing, but not a great deal more. It was simply Anatoli taking advantage of his good looks combined with the ready availability of beautiful, Russian women in the city. The outcome was inevitable, if not enduring.

Misha worried about Anatoli. They had been together on so many missions that he could no longer keep count. Typically, Anatoli was the mission leader. It made Misha uneasy that this new man, this Gregori Dimitri Smirnoff, was calling the shots this time. Things were changing and it might be time to begin thinking about other career opportunities. Misha laughed a lot but he wasn't stupid and didn't trust easily. So far, this Grigori had done nothing to present himself as being trustworthy. Besides, Grigori was frustratingly unwilling to admit that Misha was funny. There was something wrong with him. One should never trust a man who didn't have a sense of humor.

"Airfield ahead," Misha mentioned, casually. "Are we really landing on a lake?"

The outer perimeter of the low frequency airfield identifier beacon had finally been encountered. Anatoli calibrated the altitude of the airfield with that of his plane and directed the craft toward the beacon. Soaring into Southern Manitoba, he kept his eyes out in the gloom and sleet for any red end of an airfield marker. He saw none.

Meanwhile, the two young brothers were still enduring the wrath of the devil.

"You, Alexei," Gregori guessed, pointing to one of the brothers.

Gregori found it odd that even though the two brothers looked nothing alike, he could never tell them apart. They were merged with a common biosphere, disappearing into the ambient white noise of life. He wasn't sure that he was actually addressing Alexei at this moment since he knew that both brothers were too timid to correct him if he got their names wrong.

"Are you the one who loaded the equipment onto the plane?"

"Yes, Comrade Colonel. Me and my brother, Ivan."

So, he had guessed correctly after all.

"I'm going to read the equipment list that I distributed earlier. I want you to say 'da' if you pack it, and 'nyet' if you didn't."

This sent the two brothers scrambling to their briefcases for documentation. Meanwhile, Gregori started his list.

"First aid kit."

"Da," Ivan called over his shoulder as he rifled through a large duffle bag, sending clothes and other personal items raining to the floor.

As Sasha sat and watched this awkward exchange, his stomach roiled from the almost perpetual gas that he had due to living up to his bad reputation. Sasha wanted to go back to being a butcher. Most of the time, he really didn't understand what people expected of him. Mostly, he just stood around and occupied space. He often cried at night when he was alone.

"Would you listen to that asshole back there," Misha leaned over to murmur in Anatoli's ear.

"You'd better watch your words," Anatoli warned. "He already doesn't like you. If he catches you talking about him you're done for."

Misha displayed a mock 'terrified' face by opening his mouth wide and placing his palms on his cheeks. He looked eerily like the boy in the "Home Alone" movies. As usual, Misha's antics made Anatoli chuckle under his breath and shake his head. Misha started laughing too.

That's when Anatoli first saw the flashing, red runway landing light, positioned 20 meters from the end of the runway. As he made his approach and lowered his landing gear, Anatoli eventually saw the runway itself, or more accurately, the lake, stretched out before his dim landing lights. It was snowing hard, nearly horizontally, but not so hard that a man wouldn't be willing to walk quite a distance in search of the warmth and comfort of a fine saloon. Surely even this place would have one.

"Fasten your seatbelts, everyone," Anatoli ordered back over his shoulder.

Grigori ceased haranguing one of the two brothers for his poor record keeping skills, swiveled forward, and buckled his belt. The two brothers stuffed their personal belongings back into their duffels and dove into the nearest pair of seats before buckling up.

Sasha remained belted in his pair of seats. Misha refused to take his foot off the dashboard and assume a more crash-like position.

Anatoli eased the wheel on the control yoke forward as they descended. He sensed the ground before he saw it. He felt it soon after he saw it.

The wheels touched down with a rough sounding crunch and the plane, along with everything inside it, bounced several times before final touchdown. The steel of the craft groaned in response to the stresses being placed upon it. Alexei and Ivan's duffels and undergarments flew from the rear of the plane to the front colliding with the wall beside the cockpit door. Once touchdown had been achieved, the plane rumbled across the snowcapped ice which quickly brought the jet to a stop. Everyone in the flight cabin was pressed forward against their seatbelts by the rapid deceleration.

Sasha farted loudly, no longer able to contain the crippling gas that had hounded him ever since he boarded the plane back in Jersey. That was when he'd first seen that Grigori Dimitri was the leader of his team. In Sasha's mind, Grigori was a true butcher. Sasha reached into his pocket to retrieve several antacids tablets and quickly chewed them down. There was no comment on his odiferous offense; possibly because everyone was too concerned for their lives during the crash landing.

Everyone reacted professionally in the wake of the near disastrous landing. Anatoli, still captain of the craft, called to ask if anyone was hurt. After taking a quick look around the passenger cabin, Grigori reported back that, no, no one was hurt. Sasha farted again as he adjusted himself back into his seat so that he could find his seatbelt buried amidst mighty hillocks of fat. The brothers uncinched themselves from their seats so that they could chase their stray underwear down the aisle of the plane. In the cockpit, Misha was lucky he hadn't broken the leg he kept on the dashboard the entire time the plane rattled down the runway. He, at first, looked mentally jarred by the landing before his face lit up with a broad smile and he started to laugh in sheer relief that he was still alive.

Fortunately, for Alexei and Ivan, Grigori had wronged them in his accusations of laziness. They had actually done a thorough job of packing for this mission even with the short notice they were given.   Snowshoes and heavy boots were to begin each man's ensemble.   Two pairs of long johns and a ski suit were next. Heavy parkas with hoods, goggles, and scarves completed each ensemble.   Their heavy gloves were stored in their pockets for when they were needed outside.   Each man said nothing to his neighbor as they gathered in various portions of the plane to disrobe and put on their thermal gear.   Though they'd already worked out a plan before takeoff, Gregori still felt the need to give orders.

"You two," he said, pointing to the brothers.   "I want you to stay behind and organize this mess.   Then bind the rest of the equipment to sleds and bring it to me when I call for you."

"You two," he added, pointing to the cockpit.   "I want you to evaluate and stabilize the condition of the plane.   Get the brothers to help as needed, but we need to be able to take off at any time. Join me if I call for you, though I doubt that will be needed."

"And you," he concluded, pointing to Sasha.   "I want you to follow me into town."

Done giving orders and still the first to finish dressing, Gregori leaned against the bulkhead of the plane and glared out the window.   It was fast growing dark and the snow, which was still relatively light, was thickening.   The wind looked to be picking up its pace as well.   This was no night for man or beast to be out for long.

Grigori wrapped a wool scarf around his neck and the lower half of his face.   He then pulled on a set of ski goggles.   Finally, he cinched the hood of his parka tightly around his face leaving a hole to see and breathe through.   The last step was to clumsily don his heavy, winter gloves.

Opening the door, the lower half which unfolded into a set of stairs that buried itself in a drift, Grigori instantly felt the cold, no matter how well he had bundled himself against it.   The wind buffeted him back and forth even though he was still standing within the interior of the plane.   Taking one look behind to insure that Sasha was following, Gregori stepped down the stairs into a winter hell.

The noise was deafening, even though it was nothing but the sound of the wind.   Anatoli had left the landing lights out and even turned on some additional external light around the door, but these did little to light the night pressing in on them. Gregori was careful on the stairs, taking them one step at a time until he planted his feet firmly in the snow of the airfield. Looking up, he saw lights coming from a set of buildings just up the hill.

Intentionally forgetting to fasten his safety line to Sasha's snowsuit, Grigori grabbed a pair of winter walking poles and made off toward the first building he could more-or-less see. The wind nearly knocked him over several times, but by staying focused on the lights up ahead he managed to forge a path over the snow to a building with large double doors.

To his surprise and chagrin, when he finally looked back, Sasha was standing right behind him having kept pace all along. Sasha had been passing wind into the prevailing winds ever since they left the aircraft. It was only the deafening wailing of that wind that had covered the cacophony of his own gastric bombardment, which could be smelled if not heard.

Grigori kicked off his snowshoes, picked them up, and leaned them against the side of the structure alongside several other pairs, though his were the only ones made of a light-weight composite. Walking up the steps to the main doors of the building, Gregori reached out and swung both doors fully inward, aided by a mighty gust of wind. As he did so, a crack of thunder was heard and the sky lit up behind him. The handful of people within the bar all looked his way with expressions of astonishment and perhaps dread. Gregori began to chuckle at the familiar reaction to his appearance. It was flattering really.

Chapter 10: The Date

It was two o'clock in the morning and Brian O'Shay, AKA The Mole, was three sheets to the wind. He was also having the time of his life. For some unexplainable reason, Brian had overcome his natural shyness, or, more accurately, his intense aversion to constantly being rejected by beautiful women, and had asked the boss's secretary to go out with him. For some even more unexplainable reason, she had said 'yes'.

Brian had been on cloud nine before the date. The drinks he'd had at the bar while waiting for the woman to show up on time had pushed him through cloud ten directly to cloud eleven. The woman actually showing up at their date nudged him over the line onto cloud twelve. They had been drinking ever since and the current cloud count had itself become cloudy.

It turned out that the girl's name was Vicky, or Vanessa, something that started with a 'V'. Brian was almost sure of it but at the same time didn't really care. All he really cared about was the number of stuffed shirts hanging out at the bar gawking at the boss's secretary walking into the Restaurant Dubrovnik on his arm. They may have never noticed that she was helping to guide him more than the other way around.

Eventually the couple collided with a table to Brian's liking, or at least that's where he chose to sit down. The couple already seated at the table would just have to move. This time the maitre d' helped the boss's secretary to raise Brian to his feet and guide him to an empty table in a private room in the back of the restaurant.

"Venus?" Brian began. "Do you mind if I call you Venus?"

"No, not at all."

"You really have beautiful lips. Every time I see you put on lipstick, I can't help but begin to fantasize about you putting my…"

"I think I can guess what you fantasize about, Brian," the girl interrupted. "Why don't you order the drinks?"

"You know, if I have another drink, I might just end up saying something I regret," Brian confided.

"You don't say," the blonde replied, flashing a smile.

Brian had already lost interest in their conversation. Instead, his interest wandered to getting a waiter's attention so that he could order a scotch on the rocks. This didn't take long since the Restaurant Dubrovnik was very attentive to its guests.

"I'd like a scotch on the rocks. Make it a double," Brian slobbered when the waiter arrived.

"Yes, sir. And the lady?"

"Just make it the same," Brian suggested.

The lady amended her order to a glass of water. There was quiet at their table while Brian fidgeted.

"So, Virginia, you've gotta tell me, why did you decide to go out with me," Brian asked.

"Oh, I don't know," the beautiful blonde replied. "I'd seen you around the office. I'd heard your name dropped by certain lips."

"Makes me sound mysterious and important," Brian noted.

"It made me curious."

"About what?"

"What makes you so mysterious and important?"

Brian smiled, drooled a little, and temporarily forgot where he was. He lost control of his head for a moment and then shot upright and started snapping his fingers in the air until the waiter brought his drink. The incessant drinking had definitely done a number on Brian. But the effects of alcohol were probably nothing compared with the effects of the two roofies the boss's secretary had dissolved in his drink while he was in 'the shitter'.

"So, Brian, just how mysterious and important can a mid-level administrator be?"

Brian tried to stop his head from bobbing and focus on the blonde's words. It seemed that the course of the evening's conversation, which Brian had been trying to steer toward the contents of his date's panties, had suddenly taken a dangerous turn.

"Pretty fucking mysterious and important, I can tell you," Brian insisted.

"Go ahead. Tell me."

And Brian did. He told her everything. He told her about how it all began, about passing information to unauthorized personal, about secret bank accounts, and about the crashed plane near McIntyre's Gulch. He concluded with his plans for a beautiful future together, just the two of them. Brian reached across the table and began to toy with a piece of hair which had fallen at his date's temple. She jerked away at first touch, but then allowed it.

Brian looked physically drained by the time he was done explaining. He was all talked out. It was almost as if he knew the boss's secretary was wearing a wire and he wanted to unburden himself to the authorities. In any case, that's what ended up happening. Because she was, and he did. After only thirty seconds of silence on the wire, the authorities knew he was through talking and moved in.

The boss's secretary rose from the table the moment the men in black appeared within view. She moved as if she couldn't get away from Brian fast enough. One of the agents was there by her side immediately to protect her. He draped her coat over her shoulders and led the woman away to have the microphone, transmitter, and battery pack untaped from her body.

Brian remained sitting at the table, head bent forward and shoulders hunched. He began to shake, as if his entire body was becoming wracked with tears. One of the agents bent forward to whisper in his ear.

"Now we own you," he said. "We'll be in touch."

Straightening, the agent turned and led the other agents from the restaurant leaving Brian alone at his table.

Brian's shoulders continued to shake as he looked up, but now it was obvious that he was shaking with restrained laughter rather than tears. As the agents walked out the door of the restaurant, Brian burst out with peals of laughter because there was one last secret he had failed to mention. A secret that could cost them all their lives.

Chapter 11: The Confession

The strangers moved about the bar, walking boldly and not looking relieved to be out of the storm as normal people would have. One was enormous while the other only seemed enormous, perhaps because of his scars, his tanned skin and teeth, and mostly his overbearing personality.

McIntyre's Gulch is actually fairly welcoming to strangers, if they aren't Mounties, but no one was rushing forward, offering to hang up coats and fetch wassail bowls, in spite of the fact that these two men had just come in out of the storm. It was because we couldn't identify what they were, beyond probably dangerous. You see, we just don't get random tourists. Or skiers, or fishermen. Especially not in winter when roads are impassable. It's not just that McIntyre's Gulch is on a road to nowhere, it is at the end of the road to nowhere. Nobody is 'just passing through' on their way somewhere else. We are the end of the line. People who come here almost always come on purpose.

Sure, once in a while we get a lost hunter, or a scientist studying caribou— once a geologist looking for some kind of mineral deposits. But two tough-looking men, in high tech snow-gear? Never. Though I am sure that everyone was resisting the idea with all their might, it had to have occurred to others besides myself that these men were connected with the downed plane and its cargo.

The enormous one took up a place by the door, looking for all the world like a prison guard. The scary one went up to the bar, and without a single leer at the Flowers, who is most leer-worthy, ordered a vodka.

"So, Capitalists," the man said, after downing his vodka and hurling the shot glass across the bar where it shattered, spraying the moose with glass. "I want to hire a guide. Who would like to be richer by morning?"

"Oh God," I groaned. "This will end in bloodshed."

"What do you mean?" The Mountie asked, not taking his eyes off of the scary stranger who was waving a hundred dollar bill around. "All he's done is break a glass on a moose and offer money for a guide."

"Are you kidding? That moose is sacred. And everyone in this room is armed. Except me. I was having dinner with a Mountie and didn't think I'd need a gun." There was a tiny amount of acid in my voice.

"And you want one?" he asked, his gaze flitting back to me briefly.

"Don't you?" I asked back in what I thought was a reasonable tone.

"I have one," he said and patted under his left arm.

"Good." I made a decision. "Alright, you're getting your wish to know everything. Come on. We'll go see Big John. Maybe we can stop this before things get out of hand."

"So there was something on the plane."

"Of course there was. And no one is going to give it up to these guys. All they're going to get is a backwoods burial." I really hoped that wasn't true. But it was a lot of money and I knew that some of my neighbors were not real resistant to certain kinds of temptation.

We got up slowly and I tried to look affable and harmless, a couple looking for the restrooms as we crossed the large room. We went to Big John's office and tapped on the door. I didn't wait for his call to enter before stepping inside.

Big John looked up from his paperwork and blinked at me.

"John, there are scary Russians out in the pub," I said without preamble. "They are offering money for a guide and I bet it isn't to see the caribou. Chuck is a good guy. It's time we told the Mountie what's up and never mind having a town meeting to discuss it. You're the mayor. Act unilaterally for the good of the town. Before someone gets killed."

Big John sighed heavily.

* * *

Sasha was hungry. And his feet were cold in his very tight boots that were rubbing blisters on his toes. Because his feet were so long, shoes never fit him properly. The brothers had gotten him the largest snow boots in stock, but they were still about three sizes too small.

Though he knew it was his duty to be at all times vigilant, he found himself distracted by all the lovely smells in the air. Not even the seeming coldness of the people in establishment of the half-eaten moose could convince his stomach not to rumble.

Feeling suddenly over-warm, Sasha lowered the zipper on his jacket, being careful not to reveal his gun.

While Grigori tried bribing the unfriendly citizens, the pretty woman behind the bar poured out a cup of coffee, added something from a bottle and then walked over to him. He blinked in surprise as she offered the mug and a small smile. The fumes that bathed his face were warm and delicious, almost nutty.

He said thank you in Russian and then again in English. Her smile widened and she patted him on the arm, demonstrating that she had a precise understanding of what was most important to a man on a very cold night and did not begrudge him a place out of the cold.

Though it was perhaps not good discipline, Sasha sipped at his coffee, enjoying the unknown but clearly potent alcoholic additive that cruised through his body as quickly as the blood could carry it. He began to feel almost cheerful and to have fantasies that the pretty woman with red hair would bring him something to eat as well, though it seemed unlikely that there would be time to eat with the increasing hostility weighting down the air.

Now that he looked about the room with thawing eyes, Sasha saw that most of the people had red hair and the rest gray, which probably had been red at one time. He wondered if they had interrupted some family celebration and if that was perhaps why the people had been unwelcoming when they first entered.

Of course, they were unwelcoming now because Grigori was talking loudly and he had no tact. Even capitalists don't like to be called capitalist when the name was said with a sneer. Sasha sighed. He was not a religious man, but his mother had been a believer. He wondered if it would be wrong to try a brief prayer to a higher power that Grigori would shut up before they were driven back out into the storm without dinner. If he shut his mouth, they could have something to eat and wait for the others in comfort.

"Look, mister," One of the red haired men finally said. "No one is going out in that storm to look for anything, so put away your money. Sit down and shut up and try the venison. It's delicious."

This seemed very sensible advice, but Grigori began to swell up like an angry toad, his face turning redder and redder until Sasha wondered if perhaps his first prayer to the Almighty God would be answered by Grigori having a heart attack. If that fortunate event should happen, Sasha promised that he would become a Christian man.

But Grigori did not fall to the floor. The stupid man reached for his pistol, but before he could pull it from his coat pocket, half a dozen of the people in the room were standing up and pointing guns at them. Well, at Grigori. Sasha was happy that he was not the object of their anger. Especially the pretty woman behind the bar who was shaking her head in disbelief and tapping on the door that probably led to an office.

* * *

"And that's all there is to it," Big John said. "Everything is right here in the safe just waiting to be returned."

I must say that I think he did an excellent job of making the town's selfish and larcenous impulses sound almost praiseworthy. I especially liked the part about being afraid to mention the jewels on the phone line where someone— like the Russians— might be listening, and how he deftly managed to insinuate that it was the Mountie's fault that they hadn't had an opportunity for private speech so that Big John could inform him of the loot we had found in the plane. I did notice that while Big John mentioned jewelry and bonds, he didn't have much— well, anything— to say about the cash or gold. Perhaps I should have called him on it and gone for full disclosure, but I thought that we had revealed enough for Chuck to make up his mind about a course of action.

"See, no drugs," I said. "No white slaves either."

"I have to call this in anyway," Chuck said. He shook his head. "I'll put it all in the best possible light. You may even be correct about there being a Russian listener out there. After all, they got here awfully quickly and if they had some kind of location device, they wouldn't need a guide to the crash site." He frowned. "I suppose that we must consider the possibility that someone in the office might have let the story of the plane slip out. We've had leaks before."

"Aye, I thought this myself. Who can we trust, eh?" John asked without a blush. "But as to what to do— the phone is down and so is the radio. I fear we're on our own until the storm passes."

"We can't call out?" Chuck asked, reaching for the telephone to try the line himself.

I saw Big John do some calculating. Was it better to get official help in driving off the Russians, losing part of the treasure but keeping the cash and perhaps receiving a reward as well as a medal or honorable mention for thwarting dangerous criminals? Or should he stall the Mountie and hope for a sudden case of RMCP amnesia and that the Russians were really in town looking for the Sasquatch and not an airplane full of loot?

Big John isn't stupid, but I knew he was reluctant to let go of the money that he considered to belong to the town.

"What about the radio at The Braids' store?" I asked. "It might be working. We could at least reach Little Fork and they could pass a message on. Maybe."

"Aye, it might do. But that's one hell of a gale blowing out there, eh? It's picked up these last few minutes. I'd send no one out into it, even your damned Russians— though it galls me to have them in my house."

I thought of the scary one with the scars and decided that 'gall' didn't half cover it.

"I'll have to chance it," Chuck said. "The grocer isn't that far away."

"Are you having the way with an old style radio? For it's sixty years old at least and ornery to boot and Braids won't be at the store to show you. Be sensible. We can handle these two men for the length of the storm," John insisted.

"And if there are more? A lot more?" Chuck asked.

Big John and I were both uneasy with this suggestion. We hadn't seen or heard any planes landing on the lake, but that didn't mean a thing. After all, the last one had crashed and we didn't hear it either.

Wind slammed at the shutters, a buffet so loud that it sounded like a body banging on the wall.

"It's too dangerous to go out now," I argued. "Big John or I could maybe try when the wind dies down a bit, but it would be suicide for you to attempt it. And I doubt the Russians would try moving around in this storm anyway. It would be stupid. If there are more of them, they will wait it out somewhere."

"Stupid like their pilot was?" Chuck asked, making a good point. "I can't allow a civilian to go in my place anyway," Chuck objected. "You wouldn't know what to say."

"Do you mean civilian— or do you mean *woman*?" I demanded. "Because I think I might be insulted by that suggestion. The whiteout doesn't respect gender any more than it does nationality. Believe me, it would kill you just as happily as someone with breasts or a Russian accent."

"Butterscotch, I am not trying to—" He was interrupted by a knock on the door.

"Dad, you'd best come out here," Judy said opening the door a crack. "I think Fiddling Thomas is about to shoot one of the strangers."

"Alright," Big John answered, opening his desk drawer and pulling out a pistol. It was one he had brought back from Viet Nam.

"Mr. McIntyre," Chuck began warningly. "It would be best if—"

"Wait," Judy said. "They're leaving. I guess the loud one isn't as dumb as he acts. The big one is leaving too. A shame. He seemed rather nice."

"Did they hurt anyone? Threaten anyone?" Big John asked, returning his pistol to the drawer. "If they did then by God they'll have no shelter here!"

"Just themselves," Judy answered. "If they don't find shelter, the storm will kill them."

"I'd best go out and see to things myself. We can talk more later," Big John said and I followed him. Part of me wanted to lock the pub door and start inventorying weapons, but that was wrong. You never barred the door during a storm, just in case a neighbor was caught outside and needed shelter. As much as I feared the Russians, the scarred one especially, I wasn't ready to murder them.

I also wondered what Chuck was going to say in his report when the storm finally cleared and he could make it to a radio. A large part of me believed, or at least hoped, that he would do everything he could to make things easy for us. Maybe he would even say that he had found the money on the plane. But if he didn't lie, there was no guarantee that his boss, already angry from the last case, would follow any recommendations his subordinate made.

Really, it might be best if the loot disappeared with the Russians. No one would ever be caught spending stolen money or fencing jewelry, and there would be no way to prove that it was ever here. But how could I arrange this? Especially with the truth's disciple there beside me, watching my every move.

* * *

Sasha was not happy to be back out in the storm. He was cold and hungry and regretting ever agreeing to go to work for Grigori Smirnoff.

His hopes of a reprieve rose momentarily when a figure lurched at them out of snow. He thought that maybe someone from the saloon had come to urge them back inside, but the figure turned out to be a raggedy man who reeked of distilled spirits.

"Did they take your money too?" The man asked in a voice raised enough to be heard over the wind. There was some shelter from the building, but the wind's angry cries were rising ever louder. "Are they hiding it from you? They hide my money from me."

"Money?" Grigori asked.

"Aye. The money in the train crash."

"The plane crash?" Grigori asked.

"What? Oh, aye. They said it was a plane. The money is safe though. It's safe in a safe. In Big John's office. I wish they would give it back to me. It's a cold night. A man needs a drink to keep warm."

Grigori looked back at the pub's door, calculating the odds of forcing his way back in. They were not great, but that would change when the others arrived.

79

Sasha just hoped that everyone would be sensible and not provoke The Colonel. Especially he hoped that nothing happened to the pretty woman behind the bar.

Chapter 12: The Russians Return

The second time Grigori entered the saloon it was leading five other ex-Russian Special Forces members carrying M4 assault carbines in their arms and shouting orders which seemed to confuse rather than cow the locals. Feeling frustrated, Grigori fired his machine pistol into the ceiling to assure the room's attention. This action produced several more holes for Big John to have to patch. The others in Grigori's squad only pointed their weapons but did yell for those in the bar to, "Stay still!"

The room stayed still, with the exception of the Russians who were moving fast to take up assigned positions.

"I'm back," Grigori announced in sing-song English standing by the doors to the saloon. He chuckled as he swiveled the barrel of his machine pistol back and forth and considered spraying everyone in the bar with bullets.

It hadn't taken long for the team to assemble after he'd radioed for assistance from the base of the stairs leading down from the saloon. Everyone was wearing snowshoes when they arrived, which was a sound decision. Even if not needed now, the snow was growing thicker and beginning to pile higher. As soon as the brothers ran up dragging the snow sledge behind them, the party began shucking their winter gear and distributing weapons.

It took even less time for the Russians to subdue everyone in the bar, all seven of them. A quick weapons search produced four pistols, a shotgun, and five hunting knives that were stacked at the end of the bar. The woman who appeared to be having dinner alone was the sole individual in the saloon not bearing arms. Her lack of weaponry did not lead Grigori or the other men to overlook her.

Sasha was quaking in his snow boots as he moved to the center of the room to do what he did best; namely, occupy space. He didn't like guns. He preferred to do his dirty work up close and personal, using any one of whatever assortment of knives that might be at hand. As usual when close to his comrades, his digestive system was giving him fits, and now he had to deal with an out of control Grigori as well. And he just knew Gregori

81

would be shooting up the place before the evening was through. It was a shame that the God of his mother did not strike him down.

As for Alexei and Ivan, it was a dead heat as to which one of them noticed the two beautiful women in the room first. The brothers exchanged hopeful smiles when they realized what had also been snagged along with the catch. When the time came, Alexei was too shy and refused to pat down the Flowers, accepting that the pistol and knife she handed him were her only hidden weapons. Ivan sorely wanted to pat down the other woman, but the look in her eye told him that if he touched her he would die shortly thereafter. He looked her over real close though, getting close enough to become intoxicated by her scent.

Meanwhile, Grigori strutted across the room up to the bar ignoring anything, even muttering going on around him. Big John stood behind the counter, waiting, arms folded across his expansive chest, mouth hidden behind a face full of fur, but clearly frowning all the same.

"So, you are Big John, the thief. And you capitalists, we continue conversation, no?"

Big John didn't respond, but it was clear he had no choice but to be a good boy and obey. It was also clear from his growl that he was in no mood to be messed with, and that he might just bite if pushed too far. But then the Russian had the gun, and looked fully prepared to use it. The two men sized each other up quickly. All it took was a glance from Grigori to Big John's daughter to galvanize in steel the fact that Big John would be doing anything Grigori wanted, albeit grudgingly.

"I've been told things," Grigori began. "By a drunk," he concluded. "But one whom I belicve."

"What's that to do with me?" Big John took a chance in laying down the challenge straight off.

"As it turns out, a great deal, Big John," Gregori hinted. "We're here for the treasure."

"What treasure?"

Gregori was already growing impatient. He wanted dearly to use his gun to resolve this dispute, but knew through experience, most of it bad, that now was not the time for gunplay. He counted to ten in his mind before speaking again.

"Come, Big John. Don't make a mess of me," Grigori suggested.

"I think you mean: Don't mess with me," Big John corrected.

"As you say. But you get my meaning," Grigori add, wiggling the tip of his machine pistol back-and-forth.

"I understand."

"Good. Take me to safe."

"I have no safe. Who told you this lie?"

Both men knew that Big John was stalling and that Grigori would eventually get everything he wanted. Regardless, they continued to play their game to its inevitable conclusion.

Meanwhile, Alexei couldn't keep his eyes off the Flowers. Rather than paying attention to the discussion going on at the bar, Alexei directed short peeks at the Flowers and tried not to sweat too hard. The Flowers eventually caught sight of one of his furtive looks and smiled. Alexei smiled back, a crooked grin that showed his surprise at not being shunned. Eventually, the Flowers inched over to take a seat at a table in the corner. Alexei walked with her, to keep watch over her.

"Why don't you have a seat," the Flowers suggested. "It looks like we're going to be here a long time."

"Nyet!" Alexei insisted. "I mean, No!" he translated. "I mean, no, thank you," he concluded. "It is more conventional that I remain standing."

The Flowers laughed softly, and then so did he.

Ivan fared much worse in his initial contact with the other woman. The woman remained seated and unsmiling during their encounter. Ivan tried to make small talk but ended up tongue tied instead.

"You are beautiful woman," Ivan commented with a smile.

"Where the hell did you guys come from?" the woman returned, clearly not charmed with the compliment.

"New Jersey." Ivan replied, the smile wilting off his face "Is good place."

The woman shook her head in astonishment.

"And who are you?" she continued.

"Russian," Ivan replied. Then he made a gun with his hand and held it up in front of his face.

"Good Lord, you're really the Russian mafia? Him," she jerked her head in Grigori's direction, "I can see him as mafia. The rest of you...."

"Da. That is because I am become mostly American and very fashionable." Ivan replied, touching the tip of his nose in the universal sign for: you've got that right. "And you are still beautiful woman."

Ivan expected to be slapped. Instead the woman leaned forward, put her face into her hands, and shook her head. Ivan recognized this as the universal sign for: it's been one of those days.

"You alright? There is no need for frightenment." Ivan assured her, concerned that he had somehow injured a prisoner in his charge.

"I'm great," the woman said, smoothing her hands out across her face and looking up at him. "So, what's your name?"

Ivan never got a chance to reply. Instead, there was a scream as Grigori grabbed the Flowers around the neck and dragged her over to the bar.

Alexei was barely able to restrain himself from action. If he had acted, he wouldn't have been alone. Everyone in the bar was now standing. Things had suddenly grown tense. Ivan looked fearfully at his brother, unsure where the greatest danger would come from.

"Take me to the safe!" Grigori insisted, placing the barrel of his machine pistol against the Flowers temple.

"Okay, okay," Big John responded as he stepped out from behind the bar.

Big John led what was now a substantial crowd into the hall leading to the back office. Grigori and the Flowers followed right behind. Alexei pushed to be the first into the office after Grigori. Ivan and the woman lagged well behind.

Perhaps the brothers were not indistinguishable after all, Grigori thought. Maybe one was smarter.

* * *

As if my day hadn't held sufficient evil, the nasty Russian was back. And with numerous, unpleasant comrades, just as Chuck had predicted.

And speaking of Chuck, when he didn't reappear from Big John's office, demanding that everyone stop shooting guns and tell him the truth, I began to suspect that the gallant but clearly delusional Mountie had actually slipped out of the back door before the villains' arrival and was trying to reach the grocery store and its radio.

Someone would have to go after him. That is if the whack-job with the itchy trigger finger would let me.

Big John and the Russian were bartering, Big John clearly not understanding how unstable the scary Russian was. He had also not seen Whisky Jack slipping back inside and therefore wasn't certain that their secret had actually been revealed. Had the Russian again demanded a guide to the plane, we could have easily lost them in the storm, but that wasn't where this was headed.

As I tried desperately to think what to do, one of the young— and, I must admit, handsome— soldiers came to sit at my table. The Flowers was already distracting another soldier, flirting with all her might. I knew what I should do but found myself without any flirtatious small talk. What little I had had been used on Chuck.

As I feared, the crazy Russian ran out of patience with arguing and turned his gun on the Flowers. If looks could kill, the Russian would have been a grease spot on the floor. As it was, Big John finally understood how really crazy and dangerous this man leading the raid was. Big John liked money but his priorities were straight and he wouldn't endanger his daughter any more now that he understood how dire the situation was.

We crowded into the office while the safe was open. Everyone except me was stunned to find the safe empty. Big John's gasp was genuine, so I knew that he hadn't moved the treasure.

That narrowed the field of suspects. Fiddling Thomas with his nimble fingers could probably open the safe, but there was a more likely candidate.

I looked into The Flower's eyes and saw that she was the one who had moved the money, probably right after the Mountie and I confronted her dad. It was why she hadn't wanted the Mountie at the pub. But if she knew where the money was, she was keeping very quiet. Feeling sick, I understood what she was thinking and couldn't betray her. If it had been someone else in charge of the raid, I would have urged her to tell them where the money was and let them go on their way. But the crazy man who was leading this party was just as likely to kill everyone when he got what he wanted. After all, why leave witnesses?

His type is rare; demons I call them. Most people wouldn't know anything about individuals like this, people without conscience or compassion or soul. I wouldn't have known about them if I hadn't been around one night when a leg-breaker hired by one of Dad's creditors stopped in for a down payment on the overdue loan. I had hidden behind the sofa while the man slammed my father's hand in the door. I was only seven, but I had understood clearly that he was enjoying causing pain and if he found me, he would hurt me too.

No, the Flowers had good reason for keeping quiet around this monster. We had reached a temporary standoff.

But I had to do something. Chuck had to do something, if he could. I needed the Mountie, I needed Max, I needed weapons— but above all I needed a working radio. It was a bad night for anyone to be outside, but I knew the rest of McIntyre's Gulch would come to our aid if we could let them know what had happened.

I began inching toward the back door. I felt bad leaving everyone behind, but it was the best thing I could think to do since we didn't have time or opportunity for a town meeting on this one.

Chapter 13: Men in Suits

The Chief Superintendent was sitting and having tea, a tradition he'd learned from his mother, when he was interrupted by the arrival of the men in suits.

The men in suits weren't identical. Far from it. No suit was exactly the same, not even the colors matched. They were all two piece, not a waistcoat amongst them, and all two button, no double-breasted. No sport coats were in evidence and only nicely pleated slacks were worn. While tailored shirts, predominantly white, but some striped, adorned shoulder and chest, conservative ties in diagonal stripes or dark solids bound the neck. Though no ensemble was the same, the suits were all identical in their determination to define those who wore them as men in suits. The suits, and the fact that all the men were wearing sunglasses, united them as one.

"Excuse me, but who the hell are you and what are you doing in my private study?" the Chief Superintendent wanted to know from the first man to approach. He reflected that perhaps he should not have added quite so much gin to his tea.

That first man wore an immaculate, blue, worsted wool suit with a burgundy red tie, thus standing out from, but at the same time as blending in with, the others in the room.

"We're the authorities, sir. Don't worry, we're here to help." This didn't sound like a joke.

The sunglasses came off, but little else changed. It looked as if the man responsible for this intrusion was listening to a private, one way conversation on his ear piece.

"I demand to see some form of identification." the Chief Superintendent insisted.

"Of course," the man in the blue suit replied calmly.

Removing a compact, leather case from his inside coat pocket, the man in the blue worsted suit held the enclosed identification out for inspection.

"Wait a minute, I've never even heard of such a division," the Chief Superintendent protested.

"I'm not surprised, sir. We work hard to maintain our anonymity."

"I don't understand.   But that aside, why are you here?"

"That will all be explained, sir."

"When?"

"Now."

During their discussion, four other men in suits had moved quickly around the room, securing the location.   Only the one man remained standing before the Chief Superintendent the whole time, then even he stepped aside.

The little man who walked into the room was probably too tall to be properly termed a midget, but just barely.   One of the men in suits stepped forward and crouched to place a small folding stepstool before a chair.   The little man stepped up to the chair, spun, and sat, using the stool to support his feet so they didn't dangle or swing.

"Chief Superintendent, let me begin by thanking you for not immediately interrupting with a lot of foolish questions."

"As a matter of fact…"

"Because, we don't have time for foolish questions."

"No, of course not…"

"I'm glad you agree.   So, please, allow me to begin."

"But I want to know who you are and who you work for," the Chief Superintendent snarled in disgust.

"Who I am and who I work for is of little consequence right now.   For the purposes of this conversation, you can call me Mr. Black."

This amused the Chief Superintendent since neither the man nor his suit was black.   In fact this tiny man was as white as a white person could be and not suffer from albinism.   He considered commenting on this fact and declined.   Besides, he wanted to hear the rest of what this fellow had to say.

"Now, you recently received a report of a downed private aircraft in the vicinity of McIntyre's Gulch, Manitoba."

"Yes, what of it?"   The little man's comment seemed more statement then question, yet the Chief Superintendent found himself agreeing.

"You read the report?"

"Yes, now what concern is this of yours?" In point of fact he'd barely skimmed it, interested only in the location because it was a means of ridding himself of Inspector Horace Goodhead.

"You consequently sent one of your top inspectors to take care of the matter, on the hush-hush."

The Chief Superintendent felt his mouth go dry. Literally. His saliva turned to a sticky white paste within seconds. This paste stuck his tongue to the roof of his mouth preventing him from uttering a word should he have wanted to reply. Instead he frowned.

So, this was all about Inspector Goodhead, was it? Goes to figure. What has that punctilious, regulation-quoting blockhead gotten me into this time? No good, I'll wager.

The Chief Superintendent nodded his head.

"I wonder if you had any knowledge of what was in the plane before you sent the inspector to investigate."

"What is it you're implying?"

"It is not normal procedure to send an inspector to the site of a crash unless there is some cause. Even an awareness of the monetary value of the cargo would not be enough to warrant such an action. We must therefore conclude that you are aware of the other thing the plane was carrying."

The Chief Superintendent didn't suspect that he was in trouble until the little man reached into his coat pocket and produced a little black box. He placed the box on the table between them and opened it. There was a syringe and an ampoule inside. When the Chief Superintendent tried to rise, a hand was placed on his shoulder by one of the men in suits to keep him in his seat.

"What do you say we get some plain answers to our questions," the little man said, inserting the syringe into the ampoule and measuring out a dose. "Don't worry. This won't hurt a bit. Well, perhaps only a very little bit."

The man in the suit behind the Chief Superintendent helped him to extend his arm and roll up his sleeve, allowing the needle to be easily slid into a vein.

Chapter 14: The Blizzard

Grigori didn't notice the woman who had been in the office earlier was missing until he had closed the safe and looked to her for some explanation.   But there was none forthcoming, because the source of an explanation was gone.

Enraged, Grigori quickly ushered everyone out of the office and back into the saloon.   Once there, he immediately sent the brothers off to search the building for the missing woman.   Big John watched with disapproval from behind the bar as the two Russians poked around his business and private dwelling, but he did nothing beside stroke The Flower's back.   In barely ten minutes, hardly adequate time to conduct a thorough search of the place, the two boys returned to Gregori with news that the woman was nowhere to be found.

"Sweet Lenin in a pickle jar" Misha murmured in Russian under his breath.   "What a cock up. What if the drunk was wrong?"

Unfortunately, his words were just loud enough to be made audible to Gregori.

"You have something to say, Comrade Petrov?"

Misha looked like he had a great deal to say, but just managed to contain himself.

"No, nothing at all, Comrade Smirnoff."

Gregori himself finally searched the place.   In a dark corner of the saloon, he found a door obscured by coats leading into a mud room and from there to the outside.   The outside door was unlocked and there was a dusting of snow on the floor.   The light outside the door was lit.   A couple pairs of snowshoes were stacked against the side of the building just outside the door.   The building was providing protection from the wind for several feet around it, but beyond that it was meteorological chaos.

Whiteout, Gregori recognized with a shiver.   The crazy woman had gone into the storm, determined to keep the treasure for herself. This could not happen.

"Anatoli, Misha," Gregori called stepping back into the saloon.   "I want you to go out there and fetch the woman and, most likely, bring the treasure back along with her."

While Grigori chewed a thumbnail in thought, Anatoli and Misha shared disbelieving glances. It was only a question of who would be first to object. Anatoli cut Misha off assuming that he could be more diplomatic with his own response.

"Comrade, surely you are kidding. Have you seen the storm raging outside?"

"Yes."

"If the woman went out in that then she is certainly dead. We will find her body nearby when the storm is over."

"I don't want her body. I want Yuri's treasure. You have your orders. Now, go!"

There was an uncomfortable pause. Grigori was the first to raise his gun. It was a Beretta 9mm, as were the guns of the others on this mission. Anatoli and Misha were only halfway to their standard issue holsters by the time Grigori's 9mm was pressed against Anatoli's right temple.

"Stop what you are doing and think carefully," Gregori commanded.

Sasha farted, loudly. He was standing at the bar and watching the scene play itself out, as were the others in the saloon. Everyone held their breath in collective anticipation.

Anatoli raised his hands in surrender. Gregori pointed his gun at Misha's chest. Misha was the next to back down.

"Go!" Gregori commanded one final time.

The two men glared at him threateningly as they slipped past the barrel of his automatic pistol to the door. After they were outside, Gregori closed and locked the door behind them.

"Now, where is that drunkard? I think we must speak again."

* * *

In a small mudroom just off the saloon proper, the Mountie found an extensive wardrobe of outdoor gear that included several parkas, along with scarves, gloves, and goggles, all hanging on sturdy wooden pegs hammered into the rough hewn pine wall. Many of them were vintage pieces, some even covered in dust, but they would do. He turned and closed the door leading back into the saloon before he got dressed in an appropriately sized set of winter survival gear. This was none of fancy paramilitary gear the

Russians were wearing, but that didn't matter on such a short trip. Chuck just grabbed the best he could find off the wall and soon he was wearing a rather natty survival suit all in a hushed grey-green of camouflage. He pulled out his phone and tried to take a picture of himself to have as a memento.

The Mountie hated to leave Butterscotch behind, but he needed to get a report phoned into headquarters and request backup as soon as possible. This required that he slip away unseen in the hope that he wouldn't be missed and that any potential arguments over what to do with the treasure would be deferred until later. However, one step out the side door of the saloon and Inspector Goodhead knew that he was venturing into the unknown. The light that he'd switched on while passing through the door cast only a dim glow into the raging night beyond the shallow foyer. Its glow showed heavy snow, flying near horizontal, so dense you couldn't see more than an arm length into it.

Chuck knew he was looking into the deadly, hateful face of a winter whiteout. Like a hungry beast, it whipped and howled just a few feet away from the door. The Mountie saw a couple pairs of snowshoes leaning against the wall and promptly ignored them, assuming, incorrectly, that the distance to the grocery store wasn't far enough to warrant snowshoes.

Reaching into the edge of the storm, the Mountie's arm disappeared into the flurry as he grabbed on tight to the guide wire conveniently strung around town. As Chuck stepped into the night he was fully enveloped by the raging storm and soon the Lonesome Moose disappeared from sight. All the while he trudged on with great determination and effort in the exact opposite direction of the grocery store.

* * *

I was mentally prepared for the cold but my body still had a moment of panic when the freezing air displaced my breath and drove icy spikes into my lungs. A second breath was harder to force but inevitable when the time came to breathe. A second gulp of air confirmed that it made less of oxygen than ice shards. And all this while I was breathing through multiple layers of wool scarf. I was under no illusions. If it got any colder I would permanently damage my lungs. Frostbite doesn't only happen to the outside of the body.

I hesitated for a moment, trying to think of another alternative. I had been in bad storms before but never anything like this. No one without a compelling reason would be out in this. Unfortunately, all those guns pointed at my friends was damned compelling.

It took a moment of hunting to find a small enough coat among those hanging in the back door mudroom. Loose clothing would let in too much freezing wind, but anything too tight wouldn't allow me an air insulation barrier between the layers.

Snowshoes next. They were critical. Without them, I would spend all my energy pulling myself out of drifts. Obeying the wind, which had shifted direction to a more frontal assault, I dropped to my hands and knees and gave the storm my back before my face froze. The goggles helped, but not enough. It took a while to strap myself into a pair of snowshoes I found leaning up against the wall.

We have guide wires strung from October to April between the main buildings in town. They were strung for just such a night as this; though, honestly, no one should dare be out on a night when they're needed.

Unless they have no other choice.

I paused to listen, hoping there was no gunfire, but all I heard was wind.

Braced, I followed the guide wire toward the grocer, guessing the Mountie was headed there to radio in his report. The storm was so savage that I abandoned the project almost at once. I turned back, obeying an inner voice that told me Chuck had probably gone the other way, circling the town in the hope of find some shelter from other buildings as he took the long way to the store. It was the way I wanted to go since it would put the wind to my back. This would probably have been Chuck's impulse as well, or so I reasoned.

Things were instantly better the moment my face was out of the wind. That's not to say they were great. Gust upon gust from the storm continued to pound at my back, actually helping me in my forward progress away from the grocer. The snow blowing past me looked like shooting stars passing me at light speed to disappear into space. I could hear nothing more than a roar which I knew would most likely deafen my ears and leave me mad if I endured too much more of it.

I hoped and prayed that I was headed in the right direction. I couldn't see the wire and could only barely feel my hands. I kept expecting Chuck to reach out of the dark and grab me or to run face first into him returning to the pub once he'd discovered his errand was impossible.

A few steps further into the chaos and I had the dubious pleasure of discovering I was headed in the right direction when I tripped over the missing Mountie, unconscious and pinned under a fallen tree limb. I turned on my flashlight, doing my best to shield Chuck with my body as I tried to determine if he were alive. The end of the stump was ragged, showing where the wind had ripped it free. It was a struggle to get the thick branch off of him and to drag him into the shelter of a large boulder.

He was breathing and bleeding from a small cut on his face up near his hair, but that was all I could determine. Now what to do? My cabin was closer, but off the guidelines. Was I strong enough to drag Chuck back to the pub? And if I did that, what would happen to him? To all of us?

I was only half upset when I saw two dark shapes come staggering out of the driving, swirling white and discovered that it was two of the Russians. Both men looked more miserable than threatening, and cold despite their high-tech clothing. They were terrified and rightly so. Our situation wasn't good.

*   *   *

The moment Anatoli and Misha stepped out the side door they knew they were in trouble. Not only was the storm blowing ice and snow at full force, but there was only one pair of snowshoes left leaning against the side of the building.

"Oh crap!" Misha exclaimed.

"Oh crap what?" Anatoli retorted, eyes glued to the mayhem going on mere inches from his nose.

"Oh crap, as in, we're up shits creek without a paddle."

"Oh, that oh crap."

Rather than knock on the door and ask to be let back in to gather their snowshoes, the pair devised a plan to share the single pair of snowshoes by each wearing a shoe on one foot. There was also some discussion of linking arms to share the unshod foot as in a three legged sack race. In this way they would each derive half the leverage of wearing two shoes.

The result of this strategy was very nearly disastrous. The two men stumbled into the dark, arms linked together, their unshod feet sinking into the snow up over the knee. Though they carried high intensity hand lights, the beams of these lights barely penetrated the storm. Their goggles and face protection instantly became encrusted in snow. The two men turned away from the wind instinctively.

The two men staggered blindly through the snow with the wind pushing them forward. Linked together with their arms over each other's shoulder, they formed a large kite which kept moving them forward whether they were ready to take the next step or not. They fell several times and were dragged back up out of the deepest snow by the power of the wind.

Staggering through the winter whiteout at the head of gale force winds, they were soon driven upon the woman who was on the ground trying to shelter a body from the worst of the storm. Anatoli and Misha were both relieved they had found the woman. Not for her sake, but for theirs. She lived in this frozen hell, surely she would know how to get them to shelter.

* * *

"Over here!" I screamed, pointing my flashlight at Chuck, giving them no time to shout orders or questions at me. "We've got to reach shelter or he'll die." For emphasis, I restated my argument. "We've got to reach shelter or we'll all die."

But which shelter? Doc was on this side of the street and probably had guns and sleeping pills— a crazy plan had come to me— but I had no idea where, and I didn't think that the two Russians were going to allow me to do much searching for guns once we reached shelter. Since I wanted to get to my cabin and Max anyway, I opted for this location. But it was off the main guide wire that ran through town, so I would have to be inventive about making my own makeshift lines for the men to follow. With experienced icemen I wouldn't worry, but I had no idea how competent the Russians were, and Chuck was out cold.

Max began to howl, bless his nose and ears, a noise heard well above the storm. He was my beacon.

"What was that?" the shorter Russian shouted in heavily accented English.

"Wolf!" I shouted back and was pleased when they looked alarmed. Feeling inspired I added: "Watch out for bears! They come when it snows."

"Bears?" The two men began looking about nervously. I was happy to have their guns and flashlights pointed elsewhere. City-dwellers. They would believe anything. Why would an animal be out in this ridiculous weather? Only crazy humans would risk their lives this way.

"We better get moving."

"Where can we go?" The taller, more dangerous looking man shouted, probably wondering why I didn't lead them to the dark building behind us.

"My place is closest and safest. And it won't be locked." None of the buildings would be locked. Unless The Bones had been drinking and forgot to leave his door open. "One of you, pick up Chuck. I will need some equipment and free hands to guide us. Wait here for me. I won't be long."

I took only three steps in what I was sure— pretty sure— was the garden shed The Bones had built for his wife, and then felt the reassuring outline of the fence that surrounded Doc's yard. It was buried in snow, but there.

Linda Skywater has a barrel of wrought iron posts she uses to stake the plants in her summer garden. It sits right by the garden gate which was only a dozen feet to the right. Or left, and about twenty feet as it turned out.

My improvisation wasn't ideal, but I could drive the garden stakes into the snow when I reached the last line at Doc's place and then use my clothesline— I never leave home without it— to make my own safety line for crossing the street. I might stray some since it was impossible to keep a completely straight line in these whiteout conditions, but the rope would always bring me back to a known place if I veered too far. As soon as I found my next marker, probably the cedar just to the right of the path that led to my door, I would plant another stake. I would go back for the others and then repeat as necessary. Eventually the trees near the cabin would offer a partial screen and the going would be easier.

It would have meant a lot of doubling back if I had been alone, but with three of us, well, two of us— since someone had to carry the Mountie— we should be able to do this in relays before we froze. Maybe we wouldn't die after all.

The stakes were in their usual spot, though I had a bit of a battle breaking them out of the ice that had filled the barrel. I was back shortly but even that brief absence had panicked the Russians, whose flashlights were jerking about erratically to look for the wolf that was still howling. At least, I think I was back shortly. My sense of time had been degraded, like my hearing and vision. My brain was full of white noise and the cold was affecting my judgment. Maybe the Russians were right to be fearful. If I got stupid, we could all die.

I tied one end of the thin but strong rope around my waist and tossed it to the nearest Russian. My hands were shaking inside their gloves. We had to get out of the cold. Chuck might already be dead. His cut wasn't bleeding anymore.

"Tie yourselves tightly," I shouted. "It's only about fifty yards to my cabin, but if you lose me, you're dead." I was slightly under-estimating the distance, but not over-stating the danger.

They got the idea of forming a chain, but looked askance when I dropped to my knees and began crawling around the corner of the boulder that had offered us some shelter. One of them touched my ankle and I looked back at where he squatted.

"A quick lesson in wind velocity," I shouted back, not knowing if he heard. "When you can hear it screaming like the souls of the damned, the wind will win the argument every time. We need to get on the ground and crawl. Drag Chuck, if you have to, but stay close to the ground and move as fast as you can."

Chapter 15: Plans

I was very relieved that we found the cabin on the first try. I had no idea how hurt Chuck might be and needed to get to light and heat so I could check him for frostbite and concussion.

The door wasn't locked so no time was wasted fumbling for keys to open a lock that would be frozen anyway. Max would have rushed out, but I barred the way with my arm and ordered him inside. Once he saw the strangers he backed off to my right and went into his alert, hunting stance.

The cabin's interior looked forlorn, burdened with winter, though the lamp in the window shown as brightly as it could. But it was shelter away from the wind and the relative quiet was a blessing. The touch of a match would give us heat and light. A little food, a pot of chocolate and we— or at least I— would feel better again.

Fortunately Chuck was coming around by the time we got him inside and forced the door closed. I put a match to the kindling in the hearth and then fetched the lamp to do a quick examination of my patient. I saw no frostbite on his exposed skin and no sign of head injury. He moved without pain. The falling limb had apparently pinned him but nothing seemed concussed or broken.

Max licked his face encouragingly, urging him to sit up. My dog knows that it isn't good to sleep when there are strangers in the house. Max wasn't being unfriendly to the interlopers but there was no tail wagging when he looked at the strangers with the guns, and I knew that the Russians were watching Max as well.

"Hey, welcome back, sleepy head," I said with feigned affection.

The Mountie blinked and looked around my cabin, obviously puzzled. He sat up slowly, freezing when he saw the Russians.

"A tree limb fell on you," I explained, putting warning pressure on his shoulder. They didn't know he was a policeman and I saw no need to inform them of this fact. "Chuck, we have company. They helped me get you home. This is…" I waited politely.

"Misha— and my friend Anatoli." So, we were going to be friendly and first-namey. That suited me. I wanted them feeling relaxed and trusting when I slipped sleeping pills into their cocoa.

"And I am Butterscotch." I saw the two men translating this and looking puzzled.

"Please feel free to sit down and lower your weapons. There are no bears inside."

Both men complied, though they didn't let their guns out of arm's reach and continued to keep a close eye on Max.

"There is an old saying that there are no atheists in foxholes. Around here, we say that there are no enemies in blizzards," I added a little dryly. Chuck was doing a good job of looking weak and shaky. At least I hoped he was acting. If I had to, I would go back to the pub alone, but would infinitely prefer to have him watching my back.

"The situation is unusual, but I assure you that I have only the best feelings for woman who save my life." This was said sincerely by the one called Anatoli, but he was also eyeing the collection of weapons on my wall. I didn't even try reaching for them. These two men seemed nice enough about helping with Chuck, but I couldn't take any chances by provoking them. Pushed into a corner, they might not react politely.

"Food first." I looked over at my camp stove and wondered if it was worth expending my breath on the store of curses needed to get it going. Probably not. I could prepare hot chocolate and pancakes on the fire.

"You are cooking?" Misha asked hopefully as I reached for a cast iron skillet.

"Yes. We have all burned off a lot of calories out in the cold and we need energy. Best to take your coats off and let the perspiration dry. Sweaty clothes can freeze quickly. It's a bad night to be abroad. We are lucky to be alive."

The wind hissed viciously, growing more insistent and angry with every minute. I let the implications sink in. Oddly, neither man looked that unhappy.

"The phone?" Anatoli asked, but as one bound by duty.

I added wood to the kindling in the hearth and then obligingly tried the phone, though I knew the lines were frozen and they wouldn't ring.

"I'm sorry, but the phone is out. There is no way to call the pub and let your friends know that you are alright— and only a crazy person would go back out into the storm." A crazy person, or a determined one. The thought of what might be happening at the pub made my heart pound in a sickening way. "I'm sorry, but you will have to stay here for the night."

There actually was a way to contact the pub or other buildings in town. I inherited a short-range radio that probably would function in the storm, but saw no need to mention this to the unwanted guests. No. I wanted everyone resigned and ready to settle in for a long winter's nap after I filled their tummies. It wouldn't take much. The men were exhausted and I think feeling almost cheerful about their situation. Compared to what was happening at the pub, I thought they were lucky too.

"Let me get out of my gear before I overheat," I said walking toward my bedroom and the nightstand where I had some leftover sleeping pills. They were way past their throw-away date and I hoped they were still potent enough to work. I didn't close my door as I slipped off my borrowed coat. I didn't want Anatoli thinking I was digging up a weapon. "Then we'll have some pancakes and hot chocolate. Coffee later." I was lying. No way was I giving them caffeine. "Right now we need calories and sugar. Except you, Chuck. I want to get some willow-bark tea in you. That will help you feel better. I know that you probably have a bad headache."

And I didn't want him drinking the doctored cocoa. I didn't hide that I was opening my end-table drawer. I dropped in my gloves and palmed the pill box. A quick flick of my thumb and I had the lid open and the pills dumped in my sweater pocket. Thank goodness the pharmacist in Little Fork still used tiny cardboard boxes.

I didn't light more lamps. Darkness was my friend and everyone seemed content to huddle near the fire. I readied the batter, the pan for the cocoa— with pills dissolving in the dried milk, sugar and powdered cocoa concoction that tasted almost like real hot chocolate, especially when I added a large amount of cinnamon. There was a small pan with plain water for Chuck's tea. Then I brought everything to the hearth and started arranging the coals.

I hummed while I worked, letting my hair fall around my face so I looked softer and more feminine. Misha might be willing to forget my guide-girl act, but I suspected that Anatoli wasn't underestimating me, so I was careful not to do anything that looked threatening. It was hard to act unconcerned when fear of what might be happening to my friends was shrilling in the back of my brain, but I made myself work slowly and refused to feel any guilt for what I was doing to these strangers.

To ease any suspicions that might occur to them about the food, I poured out a cup of cocoa for myself and pretended to drink. Of course, I was busy cooking, so had little time to sip it after that.

"Would one of you grab some plates and the honey on the table? It is in a yellow tin."

Misha went readily. I dished up the pancakes, giving them to the men first and started preparing more for myself. I realized I was humming *Let It Snow, Let It Snow, Let It Snow.*

"Grigori was concerned that you had left the saloon so suddenly," Anatoli said after he had swallowed his first bite of pancakes.

I bet he was concerned. He probably thought that I had somehow taken the loot from the safe. At least these two could testify that neither Chuck or I had been found dripping with jewels and bonds.

"I realized that Chuck had gone out into the storm to look for some of our neighbors who were supposed to be at the pub. He is used to winters, but only in the city. I was afraid that something had happened to him. And it had," I added, casting a long look his way. "I would have been unhappy if you had died before we were even married," I said reproachfully.

"Me too," Chuck agreed readily, understanding that I didn't want them to know that he was a Mountie and was providing him with a likely excuse. I doubt that he was happy with me taking the lead in planning our defenses, but he had no way of knowing what the situation at the pub was.

"Not to be rude," I said, turning back to Anatoli, who was looking increasingly more relaxed and less inclined to eye my dog. "But it seemed to me that your friend would not have been inclined to allow me out to search for Chuck. Or our neighbors."

101

"You are correct," Misha said. "Grigori is not over-burdened with the cream of human kindness."

"Milk of human kindness," I corrected without thinking.

"Milk, cream, cheese— he has none of it."

"Well, it was nice of him to send you two out after me," I said, not quite able to look up as I told this lie. "And we are all safe now, so we should be happy."

"You are a generous lady," Misha said.

I liked him. Heaven help me, I liked both of them. Maybe the snow had frozen my wits.

"I am a tired lady. Chuck and I will sleep in my room. There is another bed through that door and the sofa. I will let you decide which you prefer. Be sure to lay open your coats and to take off your boots and dry your socks. Moisture can cause frostbite. Oh and put them up high. Max is a sock thief."

Being shoeless and coatless would also slow them down if they awoke and found us missing. Perhaps I should hide their boots once they were asleep.

"Max usually sleeps by the fire, but if you like I can keep him with me tonight."

"No. I think that the wolf is content where he is. Let him be."

I chuckled.

"He will be especially content if you leave your plate on the floor so he can have the leftover honey. But not the cocoa," I added quickly. "Chocolate makes dogs sick."

As do sleeping pills.

"This I know. I had a dog once," Misha said and then yawned.

"Let me get an extra blanket." I only had one, but it was a thick wool and would suffice with the fire. "The privy is past the curtain. The arrangements are primitive but…"

"Do not apologize." Anatoli also yawned. "You have been kindness itself and we are very grateful to you for helping us."

I shook my head and then leaned over to shake Chuck awake. He was only pretending to sleep.

"I only do what needs to be done in these extreme circumstances," I said, and lowered one lid. Chuck began to look wary. His eyes went to his mug and then to Misha's. I smiled briefly.

Misha nodded and yawned some more, but Anatoli gave me a questioning look when I straightened.

"Don't worry," I said, looking the Russian in the eye this time. I said the next words carefully. "You are safe here. As long as you don't go out in the storm again, you'll be fine. We have plenty of firewood and food. Wolves and bears can't get inside. No one can find you. Just rest and let nature take her course. Things will probably seem much better in the morning."

"Only an insane person would go out in that storm," Chuck said.

"We are agreed on that. Come on, honey-buns. Let's get you to bed."

Chuck's brow lifted at my choice of endearments, but he draped an arm around me and steered me toward my room in a very natural way.

"Goodnight," I said and everyone agreed with me.

Chapter 16: The Rescue

Chuck and I closed the door but not all the way. We sat on the edge of the bed in darkness and listened to the sound of the two men preparing for sleep.

The Mountie leaned over, putting his lips to my ear. It was tricky speaking loud enough to be heard over the wind but not by our unwanted guests.

"You drugged them?" Chuck guessed.

I turned my head, searching for his ear and grazed a cheek on the way. He didn't pull back in disgust and I found myself wondering— quite irrelevantly— if he were married or otherwise romantically involved. I hadn't thought to ask before.

"Yes. Hope it works. I wasn't obvious, was I?" I asked, thinking of Anatoli's observant gaze. "I mean, they drank it. I think."

"No, you were very smooth. I was just looking for it. How bad is it back at the pub?" Chuck asked and I realized that he didn't know what had happened at The Lonesome Moose.

"Bad enough. There are six Russians—well, four there now. Heavily armed. The crazy one, Grigori, has taken everybody hostage and shot up the place a bit. He threatened to kill the Flowers if Big John didn't open the safe. I suspect he heard about the safe from Whisky Jack who came slinking in with them." I forced myself to slow down the tumble of words and breathe properly. I needed to save my energy for our next venture and not waste time on details and speculation that didn't matter. "The safe was empty. I think the Flowers moved the money earlier when she got a look at the crazy Russian and figured he'd be back. She has good instincts and doesn't always tell her father what she's doing."

Or maybe she moved it even earlier and that was why she had sent the Mountie to me. Either way, she hadn't told Big John.

"Go on. How did you escape?" There was more head turning, but we had worked out our ballet and weren't mashing noses on the head pivot anymore.

"Same way you did. There was confusion after the safe was found empty and I slipped away. I knew you were out there, maybe lost. And that you didn't know how many Russians had come back. Otherwise you wouldn't have left."

"Thank you for that," Chuck said. "For not thinking that I would have run away and left you."

"Of course not. You wouldn't be that sensible."

He grunted. It might have been a laugh.

"Did the Flowers tell them where the loot was?"

"No. She is thinking—" I took another deep breath, slow five count in, slow five count out. "She thinks the crazy Russian will kill everyone when he gets what he wants. He doesn't know the Flowers moved the loot and he may be thinking that Whisky Jack just made up the story after all— in which case I pity Jack. I don't even know for sure that she moved it but...."

"But say she did. What happens next?"

"She's stalling for time while I find you, and then we go back and try to rescue them before the crazy one starts torturing people. I know that sounds a little ambitious, but the pub has a lot of ways in and out that we can use. And I don't think the other Russians have their hearts in this venture. If we can take out the leader, it will be okay. At the very least we can help a lot of people escape. The storm is dangerous, but not as bad as that Russian."

I hoped that it would be okay. I didn't think I could stand it if I was wrong.

Chuck stared at me, though it was dark and he couldn't see my face. Suddenly he chuckled. The sound was soft but distinct.

"That's the craziest thing I've ever heard, but I think you're right. Certainly the two out there aren't putting themselves out to get back and help their comrade."

"And we don't have a choice. Or I don't. No one is coming to save us. We are on our own."

He digested this.

"And so?"

"So, they go to sleep, we gear up and maybe try to use my radio. It's kind of like a CB only fairly short range. I don't know if we'll get anyone even in town with the storm, but we can try. I think maybe the wind is dying some. Maybe it will blow itself out. Sometimes these storms are vicious but brief, and the weird magnetic anomalies don't last that long. If we can get The Braids, she'll be able to contact your people."

This was probably unwarranted optimism, but a positive attitude can carry the day.

"And then we go to the pub?" the Mountie asked.

"Yes. We arm ourselves and take Max who can guide us through the storm. There is a kind of cargo door into the basement. We can go in that way."

"And then we take out the crazy Russian and rescue everyone?"

"Yes. It's simple really." And for the first time in hours, I felt like smiling. It was loony but I was ready to run with it. "So, are you a good shot?" I asked.

"Fair. And you?"

"Great with cans. Haven't shot at a man before, but it can't be that different."

"It's different," Chuck said, and then we both fell silent, listening to the gentle lull-a-bye of drug-induced snores.

* * *

The clouds had begun to lighten with morning by the time we made it back to the pub. The return journey was unpleasant for everyone except Max, but the wind had died enough that we were at least able to travel upright, and having Max along diminished much of my fear of the weather. I began to believe that we might win the grudge match after all.

I was further encouraged to stagger around to the back of the pub where there was shelter from the worst of the storm and to discover the Flowers and the two young soldiers trying to help the behemoth-sized Russian out of the women's bathroom window. Proportion seemed to be winning over determination, but they hadn't given up yet.

"Hello," I said and all of them jumped. The Flowers gasped and then reached over to hug me.

"You're alive! I was afraid that Anatoli and Misha would catch you."

"They did, but things are fine. They're sleeping back at the cabin. The storm almost killed them." I didn't mention the drugs.

"Oh. And you found the— Chuck." She stooped to pat Max but sent a smile at the Mountie.

"Yes, a tree fell on him but he's okay. Where are the others?" I asked, watching with interest as the two boys continued to tug on the red-faced giant wedged in the window.

"They all got out— except Dad and Whisky Jack. Grigori got angry and Jack is… hurt. The guys are all supposed to be searching the pub, looking for hiding places since Grigori thinks the money can't have been moved very far."

So Grigori was crazy but not rock stupid.

"And you all have had enough with 'searching'?" I asked of the one who had tried flirting with me. If the Russians had turned on their leader this was a game-changer.

"*Da*. The colonel, he is insane. I do not believe there is any money here in this town of lovely red haired people." He saw Max then and his eyes got wide.

"Oh, where are my manners?" The Flowers interrupted. "This is Ivan, and Alexei and the man in the window is Sasha. You know Butterscotch, and this is Chuck and her dog, Max."

I happened to look Chuck's way and his gaze was fascinated. I suspect that he was also speechless. I guess the police training manual hadn't covered this aspect of hostage-captor etiquette.

"Hello," I said politely. "Perhaps we'd best push Sasha back through and maybe try an escape through the basement delivery doors," I suggested then shook my head vigorously, dislodging the accumulating snow. The wind had let up but the snow was still falling fast.

"I don't know if he can sneak past Grigori. And what are we going to do about Dad and Whisky Jack?"

"Well, I've been thinking about that." I felt Chuck's gaze turn my way. "I believe that it might be best to give him what he wants. What would we do with a bunch of bonds and jewels anyway?" I omitted any mention of the cash. "Let's just give it to him and let him leave."

Now everyone was staring at me, even the puffing Sasha.

"But what makes you so sure he'll just go away if we give them to him?" The Flowers asked.

"He won't have many hostages to threaten."

"Just Dad and Whisky Jack." She said this bravely.

"Yes, and whoever brings the duffle bags. But leaving without killing anyone would be the easiest thing to do since he can't track down all the witnesses anyway."

"But he's crazy," the Flowers said and shuddered. "Crazy."

If there is one thing we know in McIntyre's Gulch, it's crazy.

"I will not let him kill you," Alexei said bravely. "I will defend you, beautiful ladies."

"I would not mind shooting Grigori," Sasha volunteered as he pulled himself back into the bathroom and straightened his coat. "If we must. I have plan to resign anyway. I will remain here and open a butcher shop."

I blinked but said nothing.

"What of Anatoli and Misha?" Ivan asked. "Anatoli is the pilot. How will the colonel leave if he has no pilot?"

"Grigori is pilot," Sasha said. "He can fly plane himself."

Chuck cleared his throat. He had apparently rediscovered the ability to speak.

"This is all well and good, as far as it goes, but if I may make a suggestion…."

* * *

What the Flowers and I were doing was insane on so many levels that I stopped reviewing them so I could concentrate on what needed doing.

First of all, we were trusting that Sasha and the boys were really on our side and would remain on our side once back in their leader's presence. Secondly, we were putting ourselves in danger by bringing the treasure to Grigori ourselves. We could have sent it back with one of the guys, letting them claim to have found it somewhere in the pub, but the Flowers was unwilling to leave her father alone with Grigori once he had the loot and insisted on coming so she could throw herself in front of bullets, I guess.

Lastly, we were making the leap of faith that the Mountie had calculated correctly and anticipated everybody's actions when we appeared with the duffle bags full of bonds and jewels. Grigori would probably believe that I had panicked earlier and gone out into the whiteout to retrieve the treasure from another location. He would probably also believe that Misha and Anatoli were lost to the storm and not coming back. That didn't mean that he wouldn't shoot me anyway. In spite of my words to the Flowers, I was not confident that good sense would keep the crazy man from violence. His type love violence for its own sake. Chuck wanted me to give it a pass, but I needed to 'arrive' with a snowmobile that Grigori could steal to take the loot back to the plane. For the story to make sense, I had to bring back the loot from somewhere else while also providing the Russian with a means of escape.

It sounded possible in theory. In reality? Who knew? When you have no choice, the odds aren't worth considering.

What the Mountie had not talked about as we were making plans was what would happen after the Russian left, with the officials that would get involved in the case asking particulars about the whys and wherefores. How could he say anything when he was still undercover? Not that he was a chatterbox anyway. I thought that he would do his best to protect the people in The Gulch— after all, I had saved his life— but what about the Russians? They were known criminals. I thought it better than even odds that he would turn them in.

Had it not been for Chuck, we could have absorbed the men, taking in a few more Jones. But I didn't know if Mr. Law and Order could turn a blind eye to their continuing presence in our town, even when they had turned out to not be such bad guys after all.

But, suffice it unto the day the evil therein. First we had to live long enough to have worries and regrets. If I died, it wouldn't be my problem.

"You know, I wish I had taken the time to try the jewels on," Flowers said as she helped strap the second duffle bag on the snowmobile. It was parked in a shed behind the inn. I was going to drive up to the back of the inn where the Flowers and Sasha would 'see' me. This was probably a bit of needless embellishment, driving a few yards with the duffles on the snowmobile, but if Grigori happened to be looking out of a window, he would at least see me arriving with the loot. And it would make the duffles nice and snowy and cold, which they would be if I had driven across town with them rather than pulled them out of a hidden room used to store illegal booze.

"I never really looked," I said. "Was there anything really great?"

"There's a tiara. And this broach of a bee. It has a yellow diamond as big as my thumb."

We sighed with regret.

"I'll give you and Sasha two minutes to get back to the inn. Stay close to him. The wind is still strong. And be sure and get all the snow off your hat and clothes so Grigori won't know that you've been outside."

"Yes, Mother," the Flowers said and gave me a quick hug. Sasha didn't hug me, but I think he might have wanted to. Chuck didn't hug me because he was off working on his own part of the plan.

Then they were gone. I waited in the shed, motor idling— verisimilitude required a hot engine and we wanted it running smoothly when the Russian fled— and listened to the moaning wind as I stared into the dark gray that was morning. The storm was blowing itself out. Or maybe resting while it gathered strength for a second round. In any event, I would be able to see the pub before I drove into it. Barely. Perhaps the gods were on our side.

I looked at my all-weather watch. It was time.

"Max, stay here. I mean it."

Driving even those few yards in the relative protection of the rear of the pub was difficult, and I would have been nuts to have actually attempted snowmobile travel from some other part of town. We could only hope that Grigori didn't notice this, or assumed that the natives were equipped with some kind of internal radar that allowed us to navigate in blizzards.

The sacks felt heavier than ever as I dragged them to the back door and then pounded on it with a gloved hand.

Ivan was there to let me in instead of Sasha. The boys had worried me. They were too open and guileless. They seemed to have found their game faces though and he did a good job of looking surprised at my presence.

"I have something for you guys," I said, and started shaking the snow out of my hair.

The mudroom got very small as Grigori crowded in. Beyond him I could see the others, all except Whisky Jack. Big John and the Flowers looked grim, so I surmised that Grigori had not been sitting around sipping vodka and playing poker to while away the stormy hours. I hoped Jack was alive and that Grigori hadn't done too much damage to the pub.

"You are looking for this, I think," I said, having to force the words out. I was cold with terror. The wind whistling in the open door behind me didn't help, but I left the door ajar long enough for the Russian to see the snow mobile outside.

"Where was it?" His gaze was fixed.

"Across town. There is another safe at the grocery store. I figured it had to be there."

"Who moved it?"

I shrugged. Like I was going to give him a target.

"Anyone. We all know the combinations to the safes. Probably someone who was here earlier and decided to play it safe."

"Like the man with you?" So he had noticed Chuck.

I spread my hands and shrugged.

"Where are my men?" Did the man never blink? I was beginning to think of cobras.

"Men?" I asked.

"They did not find you?"

I shook my head.

"They left when I did? And haven't returned? That's very bad. We need to organize a rescue party."

"No."

I didn't argue.

Come on, Chuck. We needed some help here. I was out of small-talk for a psychopath.

Chapter 17: Intervention

Chuck resolved two things, supposing he lived to see the end of the day. One, he would send fewer interdepartmental memos thereby reducing his chances of being sent to icy hells in the winter. Secondly, he was going to invest in some high-tech snow-gear. He wasn't completely certain that he would end up spending time in McIntyre's Gulch, but the advent seemed more possible than it had twelve hours ago.

A lot of things seemed more possible than they had twelve hours ago, when he had passed through some looking glass and tumbled down the rabbit hole. Maybe he had eaten of some local forbidden fruit, drunk too much of the resident Kool-Aid, but things that would have seemed fantastical to him only the day before now felt reasonable.

That didn't mean that he wasn't cold and also very nervous. After all, what they were attempting wasn't in any playbook. This was pure Hollywood movie or thriller novel territory. Even with the best professionals, in the most optimal of conditions, things could and did go wrong. But, as Butterscotch had pointed out, what choice was there? He couldn't arrest six armed Russians on his own, especially when one of them would certainly start shooting hostages. No matter what happened, what was done or not done, there were potential unfortunate consequences.

Butterscotch was right about another thing too. Letting the crazy one escape with the loot was for the best, if they could make it happen. It seemed that the F.B.I. was involved. Let those living in the lower half of the continent deal with the monster who resided there. Chuck did not place property— or even the law— ahead of human life. Even the peculiar, lawless but valiant strain of humans they grew in The Gulch.

A porch light flicked on and off. This was the agreed-upon signal. Chuck looked right and then left, nodded once and then he raised the bullhorn to his mouth.

* * *

It was all I could do not to sag with relief when a loud voice announced, *This is Inspector Goodhead of the Royal Canadian Mounted Police. All persons in this establishment need to show themselves at once. Exit the front of the building with your hands raised and in plain sight at all times.*

My first impulse was to move out of the way, giving Grigori an open path to the snowmobile, but that would have been a big fat give away, so I followed everyone else's example and looked to the front of the pub.

I have sometimes doubted the power of prayer, but inside was doing one long *pleaseohpleaseohplease* and was dizzy with relief when Grigori ordered Sasha and the boys to guard the front of the pub.

My flesh did that crawling thing as I also walked toward the front of the pub because I fully expected Grigori to pull out his gun and shoot me. It was all I could do not to pull out the handgun in my pocket that my right hand was clasping with all its might. Though the boys and Sasha had assured me that they would be happy to shoot Grigori for me, I had doubts about both their will and their ability to react quickly enough.

Then, from the corner of my eye, I saw that all the Russians had drawn their weapons, a reasonable response if they were actually about to get involved in a police shoot out.

Outside, Chuck repeated his demand that we show ourselves or risk being invaded. I didn't turn my head to watch, but my ears heard Grigori unzip the duffles and look inside. Then I ducked around the door frame and squatted down, hopefully putting my head and body below bullet level in case Grigori decided to make a last stand rather than steal the loot and the snowmobile.

The Russians were making a pretense of guarding the front of the building, but the Flowers and Big John had dragged Whisky John behind the bar. I was pretty sure that Big John was arming himself with any one of his numerous guns secreted throughout the bar. Someday, I really would like to hear his story of life away from McIntyre's Gulch.

We didn't speak until we heard a door slam and then oh so carefully I peered around the corner, seeking reassurance that Grigori was actually gone. It was probably my imagination but I thought I could hear the snowmobile as it pulled away. With any luck he would make it safely to the plane, which had to be on the lake, or would suffer a decapitation when he ran into a guidewire.

"He's gone?" Big John called to me.

"Yes." It took some effort, but I forced myself to me feet. I could see my knees were still there, so I insisted they function.

Sasha was already flicking the porch light switch up and down, telling Chuck that we were in the clear, and the magnified voice stopped demanding we come out into the snow. A few moments later, Chuck came into the pub. He pulled off the ski mask which he had borrowed from Ivan, revealing both a smile and a face that was red with cold.

"I think we just got very lucky," the Flowers said and then knelt back down to check on Whisky Jack who was making gurgling noises.

"Is he very hurt?" I asked, though I found myself beaming at Chuck. It had worked! We were alive!

"He's very drunk. Dad gave him a bottle."

"Oh good." Well, not good. But better than badly beaten.

"It's too early to start celebrating," Chuck warned. "We have to be sure that he actually leaves. If he can't manage the plane he will probably come back."

"He comes back and I will shoot him," Sasha said flatly. "The man has given me ulcer."

"Should we follow him?" I asked.

"I'll get the snowplow," Big John said, a shotgun in hand. "I won't be happy until that bastard is in the air."

114

Chapter 18: Skinny-dipping

It probably took us ten minutes to start the plow and get loaded aboard, including Max. We were another fifteen very cold minutes getting to the lake. There wasn't enough seating for everyone so we kind of caught hold and squeezed in where we could. No one wanted to be left behind except Whisky Jack who was still sleeping it off. I held on tight to my dog and tried not to think how dumb it would be if I survived the mobsters only to die by falling off a plow.

The snow had let up enough that we could follow the snowmobile's tracks and the treacherous Grigori was definitely headed for the lake. With the duffles but without his men.

Along the way we encountered Misha and Anatoli, waiting at the side of the road, for all the world like they were expecting a bus. We good-naturedly made room for them. The boys caught them up on events as we rumbled along. They spoke in Russian and the noise of the plow and the unsettled wind drowned out most of it, but the story was easy to follow. Anatoli looked incredulous but Misha started laughing and didn't seem able to stop.

As strange as the situation had to be for them, I thought that it was equally weird for Chuck. The Mountie and the Russians were both strangers in a strange land, and I had the feeling that Chuck had compromised a lot more ideals in the last twenty-four hours than the other men had. Certainly he wasn't saying much.

We stopped the plow inside a stand of trees and clambered down to the ground which was almost hip deep in snow. It took us a couple minutes to forge a path to the edge of the lake since we weren't interested in making ourselves into easy targets. We couldn't see the plane— a Lear jet— all that clearly because of the cloud of steam around her.

"He'd better get moving," The Wings said while shaking his head slowly from side to side. He and Fiddling Thomas had apparently followed us out of town. I notice Madge Brightwater and Wendell Thunder coming up behind them. "The ice is already melting. She'll never hold."

The Flowers, well-mannered as always, introduced the Russians to the various McIntyres and Joneses. Anatoli looked as bemused as Chuck had the first time she performed this ritual. Again, she neglected to mention that Chuck was a Mountie, but I was fairly certain that Anatoli had figured this out and was weighing the implications as we watched the steam cloud around the plane grow ever larger.

"I didn't think he'd actually leave us behind," Misha said. "The boys are his cousins after all."

"Be glad you aren't aboard. If he doesn't— see! I told you the ice would give out!"

The Wings pointed but we heard more than saw the frozen water giving way under the plane. Belatedly aware of his danger, Grigori attempted a take-off but it was too late. The Lear jet, slowly but surely, subsided under the splintered ice.

"Why doesn't he try to escape?" Big John asked. "Not that he'd make it to shore. The water is damned cold and his heart would stop before we could get to him."

In answer, there was an explosion that sent up small geyser of water and ice.

"Well, I reckon he's about as dead as dead can be, eh," Fiddling Thomas said, not sounding too regretful.

Chuck shook his head, either in sorrow, or to dislodge the accumulated snow on his cap. The precipitation had slowed but not stopped and the icy weight became noticeable after a few minutes.

"I guess it will be possible to search the lake come the spring thaw," he said to himself. "We might even find a body."

Behind him, I saw Big John and Fiddling Thomas trade a look. I had a feeling that there would be a lot of 'ice fishing' going on this week. Our would-be surfer dude actually had some ancient scuba gear. There wouldn't be anything of value left to find come spring.

"I'm hungry," the Flowers announced. She patted Sasha on the arm and smiled warmly at the boys who had moved closer to Madge. "Let's go back to the pub and I'll make breakfast."

"Sounds good," I said, realizing that I was hungry too. That probably makes us callous since a man had just died, but Grigori hadn't been our best friend.

The Russians began to look more cheerful at the prospect of breakfast. I wondered when we would have to break it to them that

Chuck was a Mountie and that they would probably have to haste away as soon as the storm lifted.

I fell in beside Chuck as we waded back to the plow.

"You know I'm caught between a rock and hard place," he said softly.

"I know."

"And you've little sympathy for me?"

"Lots of sympathy, since I know something about rocks and hard places. I have even more worry for the rest of us here in town. This is a refugee we've built. It has always felt safe, but right now I am wondering if it's Masada instead of a shining city on the hill." He looked at me sharply. "As good a man as you are, and as much as you might wish it to be otherwise, the law can't and won't protect everyone who is in trouble. And sometimes people in trouble need a place to go, to disappear. That's here. That's us. The poor Russians would fit right in since I doubt their old employers are going to be very happy with them."

"Except for me. I'm not a refuge." He reached down to pat Max.

"Yes. At least not yet. You never know when you might need to get away from it all."

Chuck looked up at the sky and got a face full of snow for his trouble.

"I suppose that the other Russians could have perished in the explosion."

I blinked.

"Really?"

"But they would need to be out of sight by the time the government dive teams arrived in the spring. And I don't mean just disguised with red hair." Chuck was firm.

"I'm sure that can be arranged. They might not want to stay anyway. Life here is awfully quiet."

"Anatoli and Misha will probably move on. They seem like rolling stones, but I think Sasha and the boys are planning on staying."

That was the impression I had also gathered. Sasha seemed especially enamored of the idea of setting up shop here and for some reason or other the Flowers liked him.

Chapter 19: Goodbyes

Big John and the Flowers stood beside me and Max as we waved goodbye to Chuck and The Wings. The Mountie was a little pale as he climbed aboard the plane, but The Wings had promised to be nicer to him on the return trip.

Chuck was going to have some talking to do when he got back to headquarters since it turned out that other agencies were interested in the Russians and had some questions, but at least his boss seemed inclined to let the matter of the Russians go away. What could Chuck have done, faced with overwhelming odds and hostages? His plan for their rescue had been ingenious and sounded especially thrilling when one forgot to mention that most of the Russians were on our side and the townsfolk were all armed. The bad guys, while not under arrest, were dead and no longer a threat. The town had been saved without anyone getting injured, and if the treasure was blown all over the bottom of the lake, well, they could always try retrieving it later when the weather was more cooperative. Everyone had promised to let him know when that was possible.

"You didn't really give that damned Russian the cash, did you?" Big John asked as he continued to smile and wave.

"Of course not. I kept that and most of the gold aside. There was also a small locked box. I kept that too."

"Good. We'll open it later."

"But I think some of the loot has to go to the Russians now to help them get set up in their new lives."

"Share and share alike," Big John agreed magnanimously.

"Do you think the Mountie will be back soon?" the Flowers asked, having to raise her voice to be heard above the engines.

"It's possible." And I found that I was happy about the idea. "I just hope we aren't visited by anyone else."

"Don't worry. We'll have everything gathered up before they can get back to dive. You just keep telling the Mountie that the lake is still too fragile to land on."

"Me? Why should I tell the Mountie anything?" Big John and the Flowers just stared pointedly.

"Okay, I'll do it," I agreed. "But you know this can't lead anywhere, right? It's a relationship with too many obstacles."

The Flowers looked back at Sasha who was shoveling snow off the pub's raised walkway and shook her head.

"Around here, we don't have any other kind," she pointed out and we both sighed.

"Come on, Max," I said. "Let's go for a hike."

About the Author

Melanie Jackson is the author of 23 novels. If you enjoyed this story, please visit Melanie's author web site at: www.melaniejackson.com.

eBooks by Melanie Jackson:

Butterscotch Jones Mystery Series:
Due North
Big Bones (Summer of 2011)

The Chloe Boston Mystery Series:
Moving Violation
The Pumpkin Thief
Death in a Turkey Town
Murder on Parade
Cupid's Revenge
Viva Lost Vegas
Death of a Dumb Bunny
Red, White and a Dog Named Blue

The Book of Dreams Series:
The First Book of Dreams: Metropolis
The Second Book of Dreams: Meridian
The Third Book of Dreams: Destiny

Club Valhalla
Devil of Bodmin Moor
Devil in a Red Coat
Halloween
Knave of Hearts
The Curiosity Shoppe (Sequel to A Curious Affair)
Nevermore: The Last Divine Book

16473053R00065

Made in the USA
Lexington, KY
25 July 2012